Treaty Brides

BOI BRIDE

SAMANTHA CAYTO

Boi Bride
ISBN # 978-1-83943-793-9
©Copyright Samantha Cayto 2022
Cover Art by Fiona Jayde ©Copyright May 2022
Interior text design by Claire Siemaszkiewicz
Pride Publishing

Published in 2022 by Pride Publishing, United Kingdom.

Pride Publishing is an imprint of Totally Entwined Group Limited.

BOI BRIDE

Chapter One

"I *won't* do it!"

The slap was delivered with less force than typical. Taryn didn't even try to avoid it. He'd learned long ago that any show of fear only fed his brother's cruel streak. Nor did he back away as Hobart leaned into his face.

"You will do as you are told." Flecks of spit flew from Hobart's mouth, the smell of beer wafting on his breath. Fury showed in his expression, testament to how desperate he must be.

Taryn tried to maintain his resolve over this order being suddenly thrust upon him, even as he knew he had no control over his own fate. "I can't marry that *man*." It was hard to believe he had to even say those words.

"You can and you will. It's the only way the treaty can go forward. If our sister hadn't run away to the nunnery, we wouldn't be in this predicament." Hobart's gaze shifted to a spot somewhere in the distance, and his lip curled in a sneer. "She'd already taken her vows by the time I'd caught up to her." He refocused his attention on Taryn. "A child of the chieftain has been promised to the Moorcondian prince. With Alissa gone, it's down to you, as you are well past being a child."

Taryn balled his hands in frustration. "My age is not the issue. He was promised a *bride*, not another man."

Hobart huffed. "You do yourself too much credit. Truth be told, you're more of a girl than Alissa ever was. Prettier, too." His brother didn't mean those words to be a compliment, and after years of such taunting, Taryn let them roll off his back.

"Tell that to the prince. You can't hide my sex from him. He'll see me for what I am even before he takes that frock off me." He flung his arm in the direction of the maid who stood awkwardly with what should have been his sister's wedding gown.

"Those fucking Moorcondians are a decadent lot. Men lie with each other all the time, I hear. The fuckers probably bed their horses, for all I know. And the wiseman has looked at their laws and ours. There is nothing that says a bride has to be female. I imagine the stupid princeling will find plowing your ass just as sweet as Alissa's dried-up cunt—more so, likely. And I'm sure it's a dream come true for you," he added with a look of disgust.

Taryn again ignored the baiting and struggled to contain the tears that threatened to leak out. He was angry and scared in equal measure. The whole idea of his marrying the age-old enemy of his people was intolerable. He couldn't blame his sister for seeking sanctuary from her fate. He was merely the unlucky victim of her self-preservation. She couldn't have known what it would mean for him and probably wouldn't have cared if she had. Their father hadn't raised them to be generous with each other.

Taryn also had to admit that his brother was probably right about the Moorcondian prince. It was a very different society than his own—decadent, as Hobart had aptly put it. Their prince had ridden in with a colorful retinue and much fanfare. They were nothing like the earthier and frankly poor people of the Marshlands. Taryn couldn't imagine how he was supposed to fit into such a world. Being the child of a Marsher chieftain mostly meant he had cleaner clothes and more to eat. His presence among the Moorcondians would be like a reed finch flitting around peacocks. If he'd been reviled by his own people, the Moorcondians would undoubtedly treat him with even more contempt.

This is so unfair! Railing against his fate out loud was worse than useless. If he put up any more of a fight, he'd be going to his own wedding with a black eye and split lip. Hobart was being restrained at the moment, likely so that Taryn would be as appealing to his groom as possible. Testing his brother's patience would only end one way, however. He knew he was powerless in this, as with all other things. He'd learned to survive his family's brutality, and he could cope with anything these foreigners threw at him. Besides, he'd heard that the opulent Moorcondian palace contained a vast library. If he were lucky, his new husband would give him the freedom to explore it.

That's more like it. Finding some silver lining in any situation was what kept him sane. He would survive this misery as he had so many others. There was also some deep part of him that dared to be intrigued by the idea of being bedded by the prince, lending credence to Hobart's taunt, though Taryn had snuffed that spark as soon as he'd become aware of it. Those kinds of thoughts weren't to be tolerated. He didn't want sex of any kind. Before Alissa had beat him to it, he'd been considering taking his own vows and living his life at the monastery. Anything would have been more appealing than living under the harsh judgment of his father and brother, plus he would have had time for scholarly pursuits. Now his future would be held by another powerful man—and one he knew nothing about.

There was no hope for it. Squaring his shoulders, he stared his brother down. "Very well. I will don that gown and greet my groom to be. If he rejects me, it won't be my fault."

Hobart's expression turned as nasty as it got. "You'd better hope he doesn't. The ceremony has already been delayed because you were off wasting the day away. If this treaty fails, I'll stake you to the execution hill myself and revel in your slow death."

His brother strode out of the tiny room Taryn had managed to call his own. Then he turned to the poor maid, who obviously wished she were anywhere else. He recognized the woman as the one who had served his sister. No doubt she was already frightened that she would be punished for her mistress' escape. Certainly the guard who'd let her flee must have known tremendous regret the moment before Hobart had severed the man's head from his neck. Taryn wouldn't be the cause of trouble for her.

"Will that even fit me?" The pale green dress was trimmed with lace, luxurious for his people. But Anissa was a voluptuous woman. He lacked the essential shape to wear such a thing.

The maid gave him a shy smile. "I took it in this afternoon."

So, others in our tribe knew my fate before I did. No surprise there. His father and brother treated him like a piece of furniture—and a useless one at that. It must have enraged them to realize that they needed him to seal the treaty, and bringing him into the discussion would never have occurred to them. He pushed back the hurt and took what little control he could. "I'll need a quick bath." He'd spent the day riding, mostly to stay clear of the Moorcondians, but he couldn't go to his groom smelling like horse.

"Of course, sir. Leave it all to me."

With his heart still lodged in his throat, and his stomach churning, he was happy for someone else to take command of the situation. *The story of my life. I should never have been born to a powerful family.*

* * * *

"More wine, Vostguard?"

Soren turned his attention from the juggler entertaining the hall to shoot his host a gracious smile. "No thank you, my lord. It is excellent and strong, but I need to keep my wits about me for the night to come."

That earned him a round of raucous laughter from the chieftain and his men. Soren was careful to keep his expression jovial, even as he mentally rolled his eyes. The wine tasted like what he imagined horse piss would, the juggler kept dropping his balls and the greasy meal he'd been served sat heavily in his stomach. If he dared to consume more, he might vomit on his unfortunate bride. She was obviously not looking forward to sealing the treaty with a marriage any more than he was. It was the only reason for such a long delay in the ceremony. From what he'd observed of Hogard, disobedience would be a dangerous effort. Only fear of marrying a dreaded Moorcondian could explain someone taking that risk.

Rolf leaned in from his place behind him to whisper in his ear. "The tension is mounting on the Marsher side."

"I have observed. My bride seems reluctant to join me."

"Either that or she is fussy about her appearance. Many women are. I believe I've spent my whole life waiting for females to be presentable to their own exacting standards."

"She must be vain indeed to risk Hogard's fury. If he gets any angrier, the blood vessel in his forehead will burst."

"The men stand ready to whisk you out of here if matters go south."

Soren opened his mouth to assure his right-hand man that he was confident in their protection. He snapped it shut again when the chieftain's odious son and heir entered the great hall, tugging Soren's bride with him. His first impression was favorable, seeing a slender form encased in a frothy pale green gown with a lacy veil covering long hair, a darker shade of brown than his own. As his bride came closer, however, his brain registered that something was off. Before he could figure out what it was, Rolf spoke.

"Your Grace, unless the fumes from the local wine have somehow scrambled my senses, your bride is a…"

"*Male*." Soren stood and shifted his gaze toward Hogard, even as his eyes tried to stay focused on the vision coming toward him. "My lord, is this meant to be some form of amusing entertainment?"

Hogard stood as well, and his expression made it clear that it was no such thing. "Prince Soren, our treaty promised you marriage to my child." He flung one hand in the direction of the boy who now stood before the dais, held in place by Hobart's grip. "This is my youngest, Taryn."

"Indeed?" Years of training with diplomats helped Soren remain outwardly sanguine, despite the turmoil going on inside his head as he tried to make sense of it all. "I was under the impression that you had a...daughter."

"The Gods called her to their service. She has taken her vows and is no longer available to seal our treaty. Taryn, however, is entirely unencumbered and, I can assure you, just as chaste and biddable."

The boy, Taryn, stared vacantly in his father's direction. The young man's expression remained passive, but his cheeks pinked at the stark assessment of his desirability. If he was a willing replacement for his sister, Soren would drink a vat of his host's disgusting wine. Then again, his brother the king hadn't exactly asked him if he was willing to wed a Marsher woman to seal the treaty that had taken over a year to hammer out. Being a member of a ruling family meant doing one's duty. Political marriages were the norm, notwithstanding his own love match. His widowed state had meant he had no reason to refuse his sovereign's command, even though he was a powerful man in his own right. This boy surely didn't have any choice, and they were going to have to make the best of it.

Still, he did try to point out a potential flaw in the plan. "Your son is very fetching, my lord, to be sure.

I'm not entirely certain, however, about what the law is concerning a male bride."

The officious wiseman who was on tap to perform the ceremony stepped forward and looked down his very thin nose. "There is nothing in the laws of either the Marshers or the Moorcondians that dictate that a bride must be female. I believe that among your people, men lie with other men routinely, so Chieftain Hogard is certain this arrangement will be to your liking." The guy bared his teeth in mimicry of a smile.

"Well, he's got us there," Rolf intoned under his breath.

"Right by our short hairs," Soren agreed. Then, more loudly, he said, "Thank you for that clarification, your honor." He focused his attention on the boy in question and his heart squeezed a bit in sympathy. However Soren might feel about the situation, Taryn clearly wasn't looking forward to his future. But it hadn't been mere flattery when he'd said the boy was attractive. He was exceedingly lovely. Being married to him wasn't going to be a hardship, at least in one regard. His cock hardened at the thought of the night to come, and if only that one part of him was eager, it would have to be enough.

Soren moved around the dais to stand by his bride's side and held out his hand. "Shall we?"

There was a moment's hesitation, then a soft gasp. Hobart's grip had tightened on Taryn's arm. Soren gave the man the kind of look he reserved for his men who disappointed him during training. It had the desired effect. With a grimace, Hobart dropped his hold and stomped off to join his father. Soren kept his hand out.

"It won't get any better for the waiting," he advised in a low voice meant only for Taryn.

Another second ticked by before the boy placed his hand in Soren's. It was small and soft, confirming the obvious. Taryn was no warrior or laborer. Just as well… As Soren's new wife, he wouldn't be doing any of that. Hopefully, the boy would adjust easily to a pampered life of being married to a Moorcondian prince. As to whether Soren could accept the Marsher as such remained to be seen, but the boy raised all kinds of protective feelings in him. He would do all in his power to make their union a happy one. When he escorted his bride to take their vows, he didn't feel the trepidation that he would have expected only a few minutes before.

* * * *

Taryn sat next to his new husband, feeling as if he were sifting through a dream. Nothing about the great hall or the people in it seemed familiar or real to him. And he knew with dreaded certainty that no matter what he did, he couldn't control how the rest of the night would play out. He'd lost whatever meager power he'd possessed the moment he'd said his marriage vows. *I'm the Duchess of Vostguard.* No matter how often he said those words inside his head, he still couldn't believe the turn his life had taken. He kept twirling the thin gold band the Moorcondian prince had slid onto his finger. Its delicate filigree proclaimed it a woman's ring, but it fit him perfectly. His slight stature had always been a source of ridicule among his people. He wasn't built like any kind of Marsher, let alone a warrior. Perhaps the gods had made him specifically for this strange destiny — not that mere mortals cared. Everyone in the great hall was laughing behind their hands at his predicament. He ignored them. He'd learned early to pay insults no mind.

And this was just the beginning of the rest of a life filled with snide comments and derisive looks. It wasn't only going to be his people who would view him as something unnatural and worthy of scorn. In the whole history of the Moorcondian people, surely there had never been another male duchess. He would be an oddity—a boy dressed as a girl, with everyone pretending that he really was, for the sake of a treaty. No one would direct their contempt toward the prince, either. He was a powerful man and, therefore a dangerous person to mock or disapprove of—and impervious to the perceptions of others, regardless. No, it would be Taryn who would bear the brunt of this contrived marriage. He was going to go from the frying pan into the fire and would never have imagined his life could get worse. The situation was so ludicrous that he kept having to stifle a nervous giggle that threatened to burst past his lips.

He drained his cup of the appalling wine that his father's vintners had produced to choke back making any sound and to hide his feelings. It left a bitter taste in his mouth, but not as bitter as the knowledge that he would soon be expected to lie beneath the larger, foreign man sitting beside him. He stole another look, as he'd done since being escorted to his seat on the dais. Prince Soren, Duke of Vostguard, was an imposing man, the very sort that he had always pictured Moorcondians to be. It was easy to grow tall and strong when you were born and raised on grassy hills that seemed to soar up to kiss the sky. They didn't have to scramble for everything in the dark muck like the

Marshers. He felt small and puny in comparison, because he was. Among his own people, he'd always been unimpressive in size and strength. How much worse would it be to live among the beautiful Moorcondians?

Taryn shifted his gaze to his plate and broke off a piece of bread to eat in an effort to appease his queasy stomach. Despite his best efforts, he couldn't stop his focus from wandering to his right again. His husband's appearance was fascinating, if nothing else, so different from his own and that of the Marshers around them. In contrast to the paleness of Taryn's people, Prince Soren's skin had the healthy burnished glow of one who spent many days under the sun. His face was angular, with hairless cheeks that were sharp and prominent. Green irises—a shade reminding Taryn of his own—were set into oval eyes. It was an unusual color for his people, but perhaps common among the Moorcondians. The prince's hair was of a lighter shade of brown than Taryn's and held back in a simple queue. In short, the man was magnificent, a feast to look upon. In this one way perhaps Taryn's new life would be tolerable.

He was also conflicted in his reaction to his *husband*. He shouldn't find the prince attractive. It wasn't *natural* for a man to view another in such a way. And it wasn't just about liking what he saw. The moment he'd put his hand within Soren's for the ceremony, dueling sparks of fear and comfort had overcome him. Here was someone who could inflict real pain if he had a mind to. Compared to Soren, Taryn's father and brother looked like mud toads, and yet they had made his life a misery with their meaty fists. Still, there had been something reassuring in the way the prince had clasped his hand — firm without being controlling — that had implied he would protect Taryn from anyone at that moment. Taryn wasn't sure which of his reactions to trust. It didn't seem possible that both could be right. In his experience, strength and power were weapons and nothing more.

Taryn's thoughts made his stomach more jittery so that eating became impossible. All he'd managed was a few pieces of bread, and the prospect of consuming more of it made him sick. Wine was the only thing that had any appeal. Although he rarely drank, this night was as good a time as any to begin. It would numb the pain of what was to come. But when he gestured to the serving girl to refill his cup, the Moorcondian turned from his conversation with Taryn's father to place his hand over it.

"The duchess will have water." The command was spoken in an even voice, yet brooking no dispute. The serving girl hurried to comply.

Taryn couldn't help glaring at the prince. "Do I not have a say in what I drink now?" He hated the petulant tone but had no more emotional reserves to guard his tongue. He braced himself for a blow.

Soren looked at him with equanimity. There was no venom in his eyes. "Drinking more than is wise will not make this night any better. I speak with a great deal of experience in this matter." He frowned. "You are also not eating much."

Taryn couldn't help raising his chin in defiance. "I'm not hungry."

A quizzical look came of Soren's face. "You don't seem comfortable here, either."

That was certainly true. Taryn took as many of his meals as possible in the remoteness of his own small room. He preferred the quiet, and it allowed him to read while he ate. Not that he was willing to admit anything to this man. "I'm tired, that's all." The moment the words left his mouth, he realized his mistake.

Soren craned his neck to look at the soldier who hovered behind his chair like a bird of prey. "Rolf, please escort the duchess to my tent." Returning his gaze to Taryn, he added, "Make yourself comfortable. I won't keep you waiting for long. We leave at first light and have a few days' journey home."

Tears pricked at Taryn's eyes. He batted his lashes quickly to hold them at bay, then stopped for fear his groom would think he was flirting. It was hard not to cry at the idea of leaving everything he'd known, however bleak it had been, for some foreign place. He wanted to shout at the prince that Moorcondia would *never* be his home. Pride and hard-learned lessons about the cost of disobedience had him instead pushing away from the table and standing. He jolted when the soldier pulled the chair back to give him room to leave the table.

"Thank you," Taryn managed to say before heading down the length of the great hall to leave. Everyone's eyes were upon him, even as they continued to talk among themselves. There were a few open titters at his expense. He ignored them as he'd always done, sailing from the great hall with as much dignity as he could manage. Oddly, the swishing of his unfamiliar skirts helped him feel as if he were armored against the others' contempt. The fresh night air was a balm to his nerves, and the relative quiet of the outside was also a welcome relief.

The soldier overtook him. "With your permission, your grace, I will lead you to the prince's tent."

Taryn nodded, even as he took his place behind the man. "You don't have to keep up the pretense with no one about to hear. I'm only a Marsher."

The soldier stopped abruptly, forcing Taryn to do the same, and turned to face him. "Your pardon, but there is no pretense. I am Rolf of the Outer Vale, liege man to Prince Soren, Duke of Vostguard. You are his duchess. I will always treat you with the respect of your position, even if I'm struggling to sort out the pronouns," he added with a wry grin that disarmed Taryn, despite his trepidation.

"You are not alone in that," Taryn allowed, his own lips twitching. Was he going to have to get used to everyone referring to him as 'she' and 'her'? Had he lost his identity as a male for the rest of his life? He was sure no one had the answer to that question, because substituting him as the Moorcondian prince's bride had been a last-ditch effort to save the treaty. There was no precedent for how exactly this ridiculous situation was supposed to work. If there had been, the Moorcondian wouldn't have questioned the legality of it. Taryn's life had become a social experiment, the gods help him.

The liege man continued to stare at him. "Forgive my forwardness, your grace, but the prince is a good man. All who serve him would tell you so. There is not a Moorcondian man here who would not lay down his life for him."

While somewhat comforted by these unsolicited words, Taryn also knew that men valued traits in other men that he did not. "I accept your sincerity, Rolf of the Outer Vale, but I am not one of his soldiers." With that said, he started walking again, sure that Rolf would take him to the right place, whether Taryn liked it or not.

As it turned out, he could have found the tent on its own. It was larger than the others and had a picture of a rampant horse on the side. He knew from the prince's standard that it was Soren's coat of arms. Rolf lifted the large flap to allow him to enter easily. The inside was just as impressive, although not overly ostentatious. A teenage boy about his own age popped up from where he'd been sitting, mending a garment. He bowed low at the sight of Taryn.

"Good evening, your grace." Word had traveled apparently as the boy didn't show any signs of surprise at what his new duchess looked like.

Rolf stepped past Taryn. "This is Sam, your grace, one of the prince's squires." He cleared his throat briefly. "If you are amenable, he will help you prepare for the night...or I can fetch someone else?"

Taryn clenched the sides of his skirts. He wanted to tell everyone to get out, but the laces to his dress were in the back, so he did need help. And another boy would be preferable to revisiting the awkwardness of relying on his sister's former maid.

He nodded briefly. "Sam will do nicely, thank you."

The squire smiled broadly. "It will be my privilege, your grace. Please let me know of whatever you need."

Rolf also smiled as well, clearly happy for the issue to be resolved so easily, and he bowed to Taryn as the squire had. Apparently the Moorcondians were fond of the gesture. "Then I bid you good night, your grace. I'm sure the prince will join you soon." The man hurried out.

That was just as well, because it was on the tip of Taryn's tongue to ask him if that was supposed to be reassuring or a warning. Either way, there was nothing more to do than prepare for his wedding night. A shiver ran through him at the thought, although whether it was fear or something else, he couldn't say. Because it made his heart pound to even think about his reaction, he concentrated on the mundane.

Turning around, he said, "Would you please unlace the back? And I would appreciate a bowl of warm water and a cloth to cleanse my skin." The great hall had been hot with all those bodies packed in, and he felt sweaty. If nothing else, pride dictated that he not go to his marriage bed dirty.

* * * *

It turned out that his marriage bed was actually a thick and soft pallet that put his moss-filled mattress to shame. There was nothing for him to complain about regarding either his treatment or his surroundings. Sam had been quietly efficient, catering to Taryn's needs with little fuss, no talk and not even a hint of derision at helping another boy prepare to be deflowered by his husband. Perhaps this really was nothing to the Moorcondians. He couldn't be so sanguine as he lay under a cotton sheet, wearing only a short, white shift that Sam had plucked seemingly from out of thin air. He stared up at the top of the tent with a pounding heart and a queasy stomach. The sound of Soren entering made him gasp.

"It is only I."

Taryn nearly giggled at the idea that the prince thought those words were comforting. He glanced in the man's direction without comment before returning to his survey of what stood above him. Too late, he realized he should have feigned sleep. Perhaps that would have encouraged the prince to leave him be for the night. But no, that was wishful thinking. Powerful men took what they wanted with little consideration for others. On the other hand, maybe Soren didn't intend to do more than say the vows that bound them for the sake of the treaty. He might ignore Taryn entirely.

"Sam has been very thorough, I see. Good lad." Soren sounded almost amused. Taryn dared to look in his direction and saw him holding up a small vial. Soren approached the corner where the pallet and Taryn lay and placed the bottle on the large rug spread across the ground under the tent. "Oil. It will make matters easier." The man smiled as if he expected Taryn to be pleased before beginning to strip himself of his own clothing.

Taryn whipped his face away so as not to stare at the male body being unveiled. He felt as if his heart were climbing up his throat. "You don't have to do that. We've done what was needed. There is no point in continuing with this sham of a marriage."

There was a sigh, then Soren said, "Taryn, look at me. Look. At. Me," he repeated when Taryn didn't immediately comply.

Taryn forced his head to turn and was surprised to find the prince already nude, crouched beside the pallet and with his large cock sticking straight up between his legs. "Thank you. I prefer that when you speak to me, you look me in the eye and don't ignore my commands. I am a soldier first and foremost and don't like having to repeat myself. And I really don't like the idea of having a disagreement on our wedding night."

Desperation gave Taryn the courage to push the issue. "This isn't really a marriage. It's a contrivance to seal the treaty."

Soren appeared taken aback by that statement. "It most certainly is a real marriage. The officiant is recognized in both our countries, and I, for one, meant my vows."

"To provide for, protect and cherish with all that I have." They were just words, spoken all the time. Had the prince really meant them? And even if he had, it was duty, and that was all.

"To love, honor and give fealty to for all my days." Taryn had said those words because everyone had expected him to. Whether he meant them or not wasn't something he had considered, and no one cared, regardless. Whether he loved his husband or not was irrelevant. He was expected to pretend to. Such was the price of appeasing male pride.

"But I'm a boy!"

Soren smiled. "Indeed, yet wiser heads than ours have decreed that fact irrelevant."

"It must matter to you." Having made no plan while waiting, Taryn thought surely he could reason his way out of this predicament. Soren could find some willing woman to stick that massive thing between his legs into—someone who actually wanted it.

Liar! As if you don't.

"Not really. Your father was right when he pointed out that we Moorcondians are flexible when it comes to our bed partners. I've lain with many men, especially when out campaigning. There aren't a lot of women soldiers, and those who exist don't necessarily want to bed men. It makes for a narrow pool of prospects."

"Surely you want a woman to give you children. I can't, and your duty as a prince and a duke is to procreate as much as you can." Taryn thought his logic was unassailable, although whether they could put their marriage aside after some period of time was something he would have to research.

Soren wasn't impressed with the point. "I already have children, an heir plus more. You will meet them in a few days' time because I have them living in the palace with me instead of at the seat of my duchy." The man's expression turned sad for a moment. "Since their mother died, I have wanted to keep them close."

Taryn felt an instinctive desire to reach out a comforting hand, then stayed the impulse and gripped the sheet instead. He couldn't allow himself to let down his guard. He had no idea what kind of viper's nest he was moving into.

Soren took hold of a corner of the sheet to raise it. "It is late, and while you can sleep the journey away in the carriage I brought for your comfort, I would prefer not falling out of my saddle due to tiredness."

Taryn's grip on the cover tightened to keep Soren from exposing him. "Why not just go to sleep then? No one has to know what we did or did not do in here."

Soren furrowed his brow. "My squires will know. They clean my linens, don't you know? They are good lads, loyal to a fault, but everyone is prone to gossip, and I will not have it said that we didn't consummate our marriage properly or put them in a position of lying to protect me if they are ever questioned on the matter. The joining of our bodies is essential to make the treaty binding. Do you not know that?"

When Taryn shook his head because he *hadn't* understood the laws governing such matters, the man whipped the sheet off and tossed it aside. Taryn was no match for his strength. Exposed now, he tugged at the hem of his shift, aware of how much of his legs was showing. "I don't want to do this." He hated how pathetic he sounded. Worse, he worried that his words lacked conviction because of the conflict swirling inside him.

Soren settled beside him on the pallet and put his hand on Taryn's knee. The touch was jolting in more ways than one. His dick stirred, and he ruthlessly suppressed it as he'd learned to do years ago.

"I understand you're nervous, as all virgins are. I promise I can make this pleasurable for you if you will let me try."

Taryn shook his head, determined not to be seduced by those words and the coaxing way they'd been uttered. "No! I won't like it. You're going to stick that thing of yours where it doesn't belong. It's not natural," he added because he'd heard that said over and over again, usually during a beating when he'd dropped his guard and let his eyes wander where they shouldn't.

Soren sighed again and slid his hand up under the hem of the shift, pushing aside Taryn's fingers with ease. "What adults consent to do with each other is always natural. That is how we Moorcondians view it."

"I am not consenting," Taryn retorted through clenched teeth. *But do I really mean it?*

Soren closed his eyes for a moment, a pained look on his face. Then he stared at Taryn. "I know. This has not been your choice, nor mine. But the time for refusing has passed. We are married now, and like it or not, certain behavior is expected of us. If rumors start flying that the marriage is a sham, it could put the treaty at risk. I will *not* do that to my people, nor allow you to. I can make it good for you," he repeated, "if you let me."

Oh how tempted Taryn was to give in. He dared not. He didn't want to enjoy sex with another man. His goal for a long time had been to remain celibate. If he couldn't stop what was going to happen, at least he wouldn't participate, even though a deeply buried part of him was thrilled at the idea. *No, I can't want it. It's unnatural and wrong.* The fact that on some level he truly wanted Soren to claim him was more frightening than anything else about the situation. To submit was to be complicit, so he stubbornly shook his head — a cowardly act when all was said and done. Soren would bear the brunt of responsibility for what was to come.

"Very well. I shall make it quick, then. Perhaps when you are settled in your new home, you will change your mind."

Taryn was about to assure the man that would not happen — with false certainty — when he was startled by the swiftness of Soren's taking command of his body. Almost in the blink of an eye, Taryn found his legs bent and splayed. Soren seated himself between them, his muscular thighs keeping them in place. His shift had been rucked up in the process, exposing his lower half with embarrassing clarity. Thank the Gods his dick was limp, but his hole clenched at the notion that it was on display.

Soren poured oil on the fingers of one hand before slicking his cock with it. Then he stuck one finger without warning past Taryn's puckered ring. He gasped at the invasion and tried to twist away from it. Soren held him in place with ease, a look of grim determination on his face. That finger swirled around Taryn's channel for a few seconds before being joined by a second one. The invasion felt strange but not painful. The slow way in which the fingers fucked him was both disturbing and faintly pleasurable. That conflicting reaction bothered him. He slammed his eyes shut and tried to think of anything other than what was happening.

Taryn pictured riding in the dry meadow on the outskirts of his town, a rare luxury of the sun shining in his face with peace and quiet—just he and a horse, the one creature in the world that did as he bid. It was the only time he felt in command of anything. He imagined he might be able to do that more often in his new home. Surely the prince would grant him some freedom or, even better, leave him entirely alone once they'd arrived at the seat of Moorcondia's power. But the man wasn't ignoring him now. The fingers pulled out and were replaced by something blunter, yet much thicker. He couldn't help tensing as he realized that his hole was about to be breached by another man's cock.

Gods, it hurt, like being whipped from the inside. He tried to relax, to not fight it, but it was impossible to ignore the raw pain. He whimpered and tried to evade the thing that was slowly stretching his hole in a way it was never intended to be. He wanted to beg his new husband to stop, pull out, leave him alone. And yet, he also yearned to urge Soren to claim him harder and faster. He hated how his feelings warred with each other, and he uttered a cry in frustration that shamed him even more. That sound was silenced unexpectedly by Soren's lips descending onto his own, his tongue invading Taryn's mouth as surely as his shaft was splitting his bottom half in two.

The man draped his large body over Taryn's torso, and he clasped Taryn's head between his hands as he deepened the kiss. That invading dick didn't stop its journey until Taryn felt Soren's big balls banging against his ass. A few seconds went by with them both lying still, then Soren began to fuck him with quick, fast strokes. At the same time, his tongue twirled with Taryn's. This form of invasion was surprisingly welcome. Taryn focused on the softness of the prince's tongue and shyly joined in the effort. The pain in his ass eased some as the distraction of Soren's kiss helped Taryn to relax. But it was still far from pleasurable and failed to abate his discord, so there was no relief. Soren swallowed every cry of protest that escaped Taryn, no matter how stoic he tried to be.

The prince stiffened and shoved his dick balls-deep into Taryn's ass before groaning down his throat. A few more strokes, and Soren pulled out, flopping beside him. The man's chest heaved from his obvious effort. Taryn didn't dare look at him, instead lowering his shaking legs and pulling his shift down again. There was a deep and unpleasant ache throughout his abdomen and his hole pulsed painfully. Perversely, there were other sensations down there that spoke of some unfulfilled possibility. He chose to ignore them and instead focused on the wetness oozing past his hole. He disliked the sensation and wanted to at least wipe it away with a cloth. But that would have meant climbing over his *husband*, and he didn't dare make any more contact with him.

"Are you all right?"

The question surprised Taryn. In his experience, powerful men didn't worry about how other's felt, and he was still too angry about the whole affair to give the man any quarter. "Does it matter if I am or not?" Soren might not have had any more choice than he, but the man was the only target for Taryn's bitterness.

Once again, Soren sighed, as if he were the put-upon one, which to be fair, he was in a way. "No, I suppose not. Get some sleep. Morning will come soon enough." He sounded as weary as Taryn felt.

The prince braced himself on one arm to turn down the lantern, flicked the sheet over them both, then rolled onto his side away from Taryn. It wasn't long before the man's heavy breathing told Taryn that he was asleep. With the discomfort of his deflowering and the growing anger over his predicament, it took Taryn a lot longer to unclench his muscles and clear his mind enough to follow his new husband into slumber.

Chapter Two

Soren woke with the instant alertness of his warrior training. He knew he was safely lodged in his own tent, heavily guarded, and with the day promising the start back to his home. The only difference was that while on campaign, he rarely experienced the morning delight of having a pert rump humping against his hard cock. He didn't give any thought to indulging his instinctive desire to slide his dick into the invitation of that welcoming heat. At least he thought it had been an encouragement, but he hadn't yet fully seated himself into that pliant place before his bedmate — his *wife* — roused from the effort and immediately tried to pull away.

Soren wrapped his arm around Taryn's slender waist and held him in place. Despite protests to the contrary the previous night, he could have sworn his wife had started to respond favorably to his touch. Taryn simply needed time to accept that his attraction to another man wasn't something horrible to suppress. Ignoring the muffled squawk of indignation, he thrust gently to build the pleasure. At the same time, he reached to clasp the stiff shaft rising from Taryn's groin. Its owner slapped him away with sufficient force to make it clear that for the time being, any further efforts on his part to help his bride enjoy their marriage bed were going to be rebuffed. Disappointed, he finished quickly and disengaged before rolling onto his back.

He stared at the colorful ceiling of his royal tent, searching for words that might rectify the conflict between them. He wanted to make this marriage work, for his own sake as well as that of his country. His personal code of conduct dismissed the idea of seeking comfort elsewhere while married. And he was sure he'd detected a gleam of interest in the Marsher boy's eyes and the way he'd responded to Soren's kiss. There was some hope that, with patience, they could forge a real relationship in and out of bed. Before he could reason a path to achieve his goal, there was a familiar scratching at his tent. The flap opened, and his two squires entered, carrying bowls and cloths.

Sam greeted him in the usual cheery way. "Good morning, your highness. Please forgive the early intrusion, but Sir Rolf insisted we rouse you and the duchess, as he's eager to get the journey under way."

Soren lifted himself up to his elbows and gave Sam a reassuring grin. "I understand what a taskmaster he can be, and he's not wrong. We have a long journey, and it's best not to waste any more time than necessary in beginning."

Sam walked to a small table in the corner and set his burdens down, which included more than simply a washing rag. He carefully laid a colorful fold of what appeared to be a gown and soft half boots in a similar color. "If it pleases you, your highness, I will tend to the duchess' morning ablutions while Tom caters to your needs."

Whipping the sheet off his body, Soren stood and stretched without embarrassment. His squires were well used to his nudity. "That is a fine plan." He glanced at his wife and found Taryn sitting up with his gaze cast downward. Likely he wasn't used to this kind of service. The Marsher chieftain looked to be the kind who saw only to his own comforts. "My dear, you'll find Sam to be an excellent...temporary maid." Damn, the law about this marriage might be simple, but navigating how to incorporate a male into a traditionally female role wasn't going to be easy. He'd noticed, too, how everyone was avoiding the use of pronouns.

What a tangle!

Time was wasting, however, and as he figured his bride wouldn't be comfortable being under his scrutiny, he moved away from the pallet and over to the washcloth held in Tom's waiting arms. He kept one eye on Taryn, not sure of how he would react to all this sudden attention. After a few seconds, the boy pulled off his shift, giving Soren a glimpse of his smooth chest, which proved to be surprisingly interesting to Soren's gaze. Then Taryn rose from the pallet, wrapping the sheet around his waist and dragging it behind him as he went to Sam. The squire, bless him, didn't try to tug the cloth away, instead concentrating on washing Taryn's upper body. Soren made himself look away to avoid embarrassing the poor Marsher unnecessarily. He could still hear him, though.

"I'll do that, thank you." Taryn's voice was low, yet steady. However he might be feeling, he was good at hiding it.

Hard lessons learned being Hogard's son.

"Of course, your grace." There was a rustling of cloth. "This is your traveling gown, your grace, part of the trousseau the dowager queen sent as a wedding gift. I, um, took the liberty of altering it last night to, ah, fit you better."

"That was very thoughtful. Thank you."

Taryn's kindness to a lowly squire was a good sign. Soren always judged people by how they treated those beneath them. Taryn must detest the idea of wearing a dress as he traveled, but he wasn't taking out his unhappiness about that, or anything else, on someone wholly blameless of the situation. Soren would be another matter. His bride didn't seem to hesitate to cast him in the role of villain, if last night and this morning were any indication.

And he's not wrong. Soren knew a stab of guilt. His reasons notwithstanding, he'd hurt Taryn on a number of fronts, and while Soren was determined to make the marriage work, he needed to tread more carefully as he wooed his bride.

"I hope these boots fit, your grace. They seem about the right size."

"It doesn't matter. They'll do well enough to keep my feet in the stirrups."

"Oh, um..." Sam went silent, obviously not comfortable in correcting his duchess.

In the act of pulling his tunic over his head, Soren realized this duty fell to him. "You will not be riding," he said, busying himself with pulling on his trousers.

"We brought a carriage to make your journey back to Moorcondia. I believe I mentioned that last night."

"I don't need a carriage!" Taryn's meek demeanor was gone and now the air filled with tension.

Soren plastered a patient smile on his face before turning to confront his bride. Taryn stood staring at the ground with clenched fists by his side. For a moment, Soren was distracted by how fetching the boy looked in the soft blue gown bordered with intricate flowers along the bodice, cuffs and hem. "The carriage is a gift from my brother, the king. He would have his new sister-in-law travel in as much comfort as he can provide. I will be setting a fast pace. You'll come to appreciate your mode of travel by the day's end, I'll wager."

Taryn lifted his gaze, letting Soren see the depths of his anger and resentment for a few seconds before addressing Sam. "Those boots are very fine, indeed. I'm sure I'll find them to my liking more than my old ones." Once again, he treated the squire with courtesy, not unleashing his emotions on someone who couldn't fight back.

Soren felt the tension leave the tent, his squires visibly relaxing from Taryn's efforts to diffuse the situation. The fact that his bride was so good at it made Soren both sad and furious. This was a long-honed skill, of that, he was sure. And that meant Taryn had grown up learning to placate powerful men. Nevertheless, the boy hadn't become hardened or mean from the experience. He'd kept his innate…sweetness, Soren supposed, although reserved apparently for those *not* his husband. Nevertheless, it endeared his bride to him even more.

And I am not helping this situation by lingering.

Soren quickly finished dressing and told no one in particular, "I will break my fast at the cook's wagon. See that a meal is brought here for the duchess." He doubted Taryn would want to tramp through the now-muddy encampment, dressed as he was.

Tom bowed. "Of course, your highness."

Satisfied that his bride was in good hands, Soren left the tent and strode to his destination. As he went, Rolf came into view, shouting orders to the men to hasten their departure. The efficient commander then joined Soren.

"We're nearly ready, your highness. Breaking down your tent is the last major task before we can begin our journey home. I, for one, can't wait to see the back of this place."

Soren knew he should admonish the man for disrespecting a new ally, but as his own view was the same, he didn't bother with trying to be politically correct on the matter. "Good. The tent will have to wait until my duchess has had a chance to eat. I want" —*her? him?*—"my bride to be as comfortable as possible. Eating breakfast while in a carriage would be messy and potentially nauseating."

"Certainly, your highness. The duchess' well-being is paramount. There isn't a man here who wouldn't gladly give his life in service to that cause."

Good man that he was, Rolf was conveying that the strange circumstances of the marriage had been accepted by the rank and file without trouble. Not that any of them would dare to do anything overtly disrespectful to their prince's wife, but it was nice to know Taryn wouldn't be the target of any backhanded contempt.

They reached the cook's wagon, and the man's young apprentice handed Soren a thick slab of bread topped by sharp cheese without being told. He was something of a creature of habit, and this was the food he liked to start his day with while on campaign. Not that this was a war situation, although it could have easily turned into one. They had come ready to battle their way home if need be. But Taryn had prevented that eventuality, and for that reason alone, Soren and his men should be grateful to the Marsher.

Soren took the offering with barely a hitch to his stride. "Good lad." He ate while he made his way to the front of Hogard's longhouse. "Gods, I hate diplomacy," he confessed to Rolf between mouthfuls. Not that he was revealing a great truth about himself. Rolf certainly already knew this. They were both soldiers and well-suited to it. Neither of them had any interest or skill in politicking.

"It would be a terrible breach of etiquette to not bid your new father-in-law goodbye."

Soren nearly choked. He hadn't really thought about how he was now personally bound to that vile man. As they got closer to their destination, he could see the Marsher chieftain standing outside with his odious heir. The two of them wore the same clothing as they had the previous night and were drinking tankards of ale. It didn't seem to bother either of them how the liquid dripped down their bushy beards. Because the wedding itself had been such a shock, he hadn't really appreciated how the smooth-cheeked and beautiful Taryn was nothing like his male relatives. Soren was a lucky bastard indeed that his bride didn't repulse him.

He quickly finished his food and came to a stop several arm's-lengths away from his host. With the wind blowing toward him, his sense of smell demanded the precaution. "Good morning, my lord."

Hogard grinned, exposing his rotted teeth. "Ah, my son by marriage. Getting a late start to the day, heh?" The grin turned into a leer. "Can I assume that the wedding night was satisfactory and the treaty stands?"

Soren called upon his battle-honed skill of hiding his emotions, even though he really wanted to plant his fist in the man's face. "Of course, the treaty stands."

Taryn's brother pushed his way into the conversation. "So the little cunt offered up his ass nicely, did he? I'm sure it was his greatest hope come true and a tighter hole for your cock than any pussy would be." The muck toad had the temerity to chuckle.

Soren's control didn't stand against this baiting, and he didn't want it to. He took a few steps to lean right into Hobart's face, the stench of the man notwithstanding. Soren's height gave him the advantage over the shorter Marsher. "Do not *ever* speak of my wife in such disrespectful terms. Am I making myself clear?" He let the asshole see his own death in Soren's eyes and was gratified when Hobart backed up with obvious fear.

"I-I meant nothing by it."

"Oh, I think we both know that's a lie." He reined in his temper and turned his attention back to Hogard. "Thank you for your hospitality. Rest assured that Taryn will be treated to all that befits the consort of a Moorcondian prince."

Hogard didn't bother to hide his disinterest in his son's future. Soren left him saying no more, eager to put the Marsher chieftain and his spawn as far behind him as he could.

"Crack the whip, Rolf. I want out of this fetid swamp as soon as possible."

"Understood, your highness." Rolf peeled off and began shouting orders.

Knowing Taryn's lingering over breakfast would be the biggest impediment to their haste, Soren headed back to his tent. He was pleasantly surprised to find that men were breaking it down. Taryn stood at the back of the carriage that was hitched and ready to leave as soon as its passenger got in. One of the Marsher servants was hoisting a battered trunk onto the luggage cart at the back. By the time Soren reached them, Taryn had opened the trunk and was peering inside.

"What is this?" He tried to keep his tone conversational.

Taryn still visibly started at the question and glanced at him with banked anger. "These are my belongings."

Soren sighed inwardly at his wife's continued distrust and dislike of him and looked over the boy's shoulders. There was a pathetic pile of worn clothing packed next to a few books. Soren put a little distance between himself and Taryn, so as not to crowd him. "Do you have any sentimental attachment to any of your clothes?"

Taryn gave him a look that clearly questioned Soren's sanity. "Of course not."

Soren gestured to the Marsher servant. "Take them out and give them to someone in need." To Taryn, he added, "As my wife, you will have the finest...garments." He continued to struggle with the proper words for his unusual situation. Just because Taryn wore the dresses from the dowager queen didn't mean he wanted to. Soren wasn't sure what his wife would ultimately choose for clothing, nor could he predict what kind the court would expect from his male bride.

Taryn didn't object to the removal of what was really little more than rags, but he gasped and lunged forward when a small, wooden figure dropped from the folds of cloth. He caught it and hugged it close to his chest, as if guarding it from being taken.

"What is that?" Soren used as gentle a tone as he knew how, his question purely one of curiosity, and he didn't want his bride to worry.

It didn't help. Taryn looked at him with determination. "It's nothing, just something my mother carved for me when I was little."

"Your mother?" Soren couldn't imagine his own making figures from any material, let alone wood. She'd barely done needlepoint during her too-short life, a craft enjoyed with marvelous results from many ladies at court. "May I see?" He didn't reach for it, opting instead to fold his arms to show he wasn't trying to take it.

After a moment's hesitation, Taryn held it up. The figure was a bird with wings spread wide and done with such fine detail that Soren could imagine it to be real and taking flight.

"Exquisite. Did she teach you?"

Taryn's eyes became moist. "No. The chieftain said it was not a fitting pastime for his son."

Soren allowed himself to consider for a brief moment how much the treaty would suffer if he returned to the longhouse and beat Hogard into the mud. Probably a lot, and as a prince, he'd learned long ago that he couldn't indulge his every whim.

He turned to Sam, who had been assigned the duty to travel with the duchess and hovered nearby. "Find something suitably protective to wrap my wife's treasured possession for the journey."

"Yes, your highness." Sam took off, likely happy to have something to do elsewhere. As with earlier, tension filled the air.

Soren jutted his chin toward the trunk. "Is there anything else in there that you wish to protect?"

"There are only my books. They'll be fine in the trunk. I can keep them, can I not?" Once more, his bride looked at him with a mixture of defiance and fear.

Soren wanted to wipe away both of those expressions. "Certainly." He tried for a reassuring smile and figured he failed. "Perhaps you should take one of them to occupy your time during the journey."

"I intended to."

"Excellent." A thought occurred to him, one that he believed Taryn would appreciate. "There is an old and extensive library at the palace. The Master of Books will be happy to give you a tour any time, I'm sure, and they are available for members of the court to borrow as much as they wish."

Finally, Taryn's expression changed. His face didn't exactly light up, but his joy showed through enough to be seen. "I've heard of it and am gratified to know I can avail myself of it."

Soren smiled at the response. "As my duchess, there will be very little you can't have. I hope you will be happy in your new home." Taryn dropped his gaze and said nothing. It was perhaps too much to expect, but the unguarded reaction over the library was very reassuring. And because Soren felt a sudden urge to kiss his bride, he backed off quickly. "I'll leave you to finish your packing for the journey."

He wheeled around and almost ran from the temptation of putting his wife into the carriage for entirely different reasons than traveling. He needed to busy himself with the duties of his station and as commander of his men. Lengthening his stride, he shouted, "Rolf!"

* * * *

"We are making good progress, your highness. And my scouts ahead and behind us have reported no sign of ambush or of anyone tailing us."

Soren glanced at Rolf, who somehow always managed to flank him without allowing his horse to pull even with Soren's. It was an admirable skill to have such control over a warhorse, and while Soren didn't give a rat's ass if his second in command rode side-by-side, he knew the man was a stickler for propriety. Even in their most drunken states, he'd never once addressed Soren in a familiar way.

"I am relieved to hear it. I don't want to think ill of my new father-in-law..."

"But you wouldn't be surprised if the entire treaty, wedding and all, is one giant ruse to take a Moorcondian prince hostage."

"Exactly."

"Hmm. Having now met the man, I'm not sure he's clever enough to plan such a feat."

"Perhaps not, but he has a certain cunning and is stupid enough to think it would work. We will stay vigilant, and I'm glad our somewhat late start won't keep us from joining the rest of the men."

A good commander always considered the possibilities. He and the king were well-honed fighting men. Another contingent of soldiers had left the palace a day after Soren and was waiting in a strategic spot to either accompany their new duchess home or to fight to get their prince out of trouble. Either way, knowing their size would double by nightfall was reassuring.

And thinking of his bride, Soren's cock rallied from its bored slumber and his spirits lifted. It was as if he were in the first throes of a romantic crush, feelings he hadn't had since he was a young man. He had to resist the temptation to turn his head to glimpse the carriage in which his wife rode. There was no way to see inside, naturally, but the urge to look was strong. The desire to halt the march, change places with Sam and cuddle his wife *and more* was even stronger. He rather enjoyed the impulse, and the anticipation it built in him. It wasn't necessary for him to want Taryn, but Soren liked that he did. Their marriage could be a good one—if he managed to convince the boy that sex between two men was nothing to fear or be ashamed of. He would have to strive to make Taryn's life a good one to help break down the wariness and distrust he saw in the boy's eyes.

"I have been thinking. The women picked by the queen to serve as my bride's maids aren't going to be appropriate under the unexpected circumstances. I'm sure Taryn would feel more comfortable with another boy, at least for purposes of tending to his more personal needs. That young cousin of yours still serves as a page at the palace, does he not?"

"Indeed, your highness. Kexen has settled in well and appears to thrive. I doubt he will ever return to the family farm. In truth, he was never suited for country life."

"And he's a cheery lad, as I recall from our one meeting."

"He is, yes. Kexen was born with a smile on his lips and is almost entirely unflappable. I believe he is well-liked among the palace servants."

"Do you think he'd be willing to serve as the duchess' personal maid for bathing and dressing purposes?"

"As he is a biddable lad, he will do as he is told. But in this case, I believe he would relish the opportunity. Not only will it raise his status, but he has always had an interest in clothing. When not in livery, his sartorial choices are quite…eye-catching."

Soren chuckled. Knowing his right-hand man as he did, the understatement spoke volumes about his cousin's choices in how to dress. That might prove to be exactly what Taryn needed. No one had a map of what a male duchess was supposed to wear, and from what he'd seen so far, he doubted his bride would welcome being clothed as a woman for the rest of his days.

"Then that is one problem solved. See to the arrangements as soon as we arrive."

"Yes, your highness."

Now Soren did give in to the desire to turn and look at the carriage. There were a dozen men between him and it, so that if they were attacked, his bride would have instant protection. And of course, there was nothing to see but the carriage itself, horses and outriders. Still, his mind pictured Taryn sitting on the plush seat, maybe reading. He wanted to see the boy for himself to make sure he was comfortable. Plus, it was time for a break in their journey.

Yes, that all sounds logical. Too bad you can't fool yourself into believing it. His hard cock agreed with his decision, found it perfectly reasonable, but that dumb and traitorous thing couldn't be trusted. It had only one agenda, always.

"I'm sure the duchess could use a brief break about now, and if we're not being followed, there should be no harm in it. The men can relieve themselves at will, but the carriage is a big impediment in that regard."

"Understood, your highness." Rolf peeled away and issued the order to halt.

Dozens of men and horses couldn't stop immediately, however, so it took some time to bring everyone and everything to a standstill. Soren capitalized on that fact to circle back to his bride. By the time the driver had stopped the carriage, Soren was positioned to dismount, hand the reins to a soldier and open the carriage door himself. He found Taryn blinking and yawning.

"What is going on? Is there trouble?" Taryn straightened in his seat and whipped his gaze around.

That was a telling sign. He expected trouble from his father, probably because he knew the man well—or maybe because he was part of some nefarious plan? No, Soren dismissed that thought in an instant. Taryn's expression held real fear.

"All is well." Soren kept his tone soothing. "We are merely taking a short break. Come... You can stretch your legs and relieve yourself." He held out his hand.

After a moment's hesitation, Taryn took it and let Soren help him down from the carriage. The moment the boy's feet touched the ground, however, he snatched his hand back. After scanning his surroundings, Taryn headed into the woods. Soren trailed after him, keeping him in sight without hovering.

Taryn stopped beside a tree. "I don't need an escort for this," he said with his back to him.

Soren couldn't suppress a chuckle. "I am aware, but these woods are known to harbor brigands. I can't let you out of my sight."

Taryn *hmphed* as he lifted his skirts. Soren could appreciate how his grandmother had chosen a practical traveling dress. While very pretty, it was also lacking in the wide, voluminous layers that the ladies of the palace favored. It made this activity easier for his bride. It also gave Soren a glimpse of a well-trimmed calf, which shouldn't have caught his attention at all—yet somehow did. It reminded him of how little of his bride's body he'd actually seen, and for so long as they traveled, he wouldn't have an opportunity to unwrap what was becoming a delectable package.

His dick pulsed in physical emphasis of his thoughts. He approached Taryn just as the boy was shaking out his skirts. As the boy turned, Soren was right there to clasp him by the shoulders and back him against the tree. His bride looked up at him with wide eyes and a hint of resentment laced with fear. He hated seeing both, but the latter at least he could tackle. Slowly, he lowered his mouth toward Taryn's lips. He wanted his bride to see what was coming and to know it wasn't intended to be an assault.

The boy's lips were soft and delicious. The previous night, he'd used kissing to distract his bride from the pain of penetration. And as his focus had been to finish as quickly as possible, he hadn't been able to appreciate this simple claiming. Now, he gave all his attention to the feel of Taryn's mouth, and when he prodded with his tongue, the taste of it. Taryn stood stiff in his arms at first. As Soren deepened the kiss, that changed. The boy relaxed enough for Soren to angle his head to claim his mouth even more.

He slid his hands up to his bride's neck, then cupped his face. Instinctively, he moved closer until their bodies touched. That's when Taryn jerked and tore himself from Soren's grasp. The boy's chest heaved with deep breaths, and there was that combination of feelings that Soren hated to see on his bride's face. He tried to kiss him again, but Taryn evaded him.

"Don't."

"I only mean to kiss you." It was mostly the truth, although his hard dick, something Taryn had surely felt, was contesting that assertion.

"That's not true." Taryn's gaze slid to the side. "We need to return. What will your men think if we linger out here?"

"They will think we, as a newly married couple, are enjoying each other's company."

Taryn grimaced. "I will not be the butt of their lewd jokes."

"No one would dare disrespect you, and what kidding they do among themselves will be good-natured. My men are loyal to me and now devoted to you." Soren tried to take his bride in hand once more and was rebuffed again.

"Then how about this— I'm too sore. The carriage makes for any easier place to sit than a saddle, but your...attention has caused me discomfort that hasn't abated."

Soren wasn't surprised by this news and inwardly cursed himself for not being sensitive enough to his bride's needs. Things were a little different this time around with his marriage, and he had to adjust his expectations accordingly.

"That is another matter entirely, my dear." He took hold of one of Taryn's hands, no easy feat, given how the boy tried to evade him. Then he led him over to a large nearby rock and perched himself on top of it. He drew Taryn into the space between his legs. "There are other ways for us to give each other pleasure."

Taryn threw him a mulish look. "What do you mean?"

"Kneel down and I'll show you." Again there was resistance, although not outright rebellion. It took little effort to put his bride where he wanted. Lifting his tunic, he clasped his erection through his trousers. "You can see how much I want you, and I won't apologize for that. I am a man of lustful appetites, and it's rare for me to go more than a day without sexual release."

Fury burned in Taryn's eyes. "Wasn't this morning enough for you?"

"Frankly, no." He cupped his bride's face with his other hand. "I want you, Taryn. That is a good thing in a marriage."

"But I don't want you! Doesn't that mean anything?"

"Yes, it does, except I'm not sure you're telling me the truth. Look down, my dear."

Taryn's gaze didn't budge. "I don't need to."

"You feel your own arousal, do you not?" When Taryn failed to answer, Soren did it for him. "You must.

I can see it, given how thin your shift and dress are. You don't dislike my touch, do you?"

A shudder racked the boy's frame before he answered. "The kissing was nice."

Soren grinned. "There now... That's not so bad, is it?" He worked the lacings of his trousers to free his dick. It sprang forward in eagerness. "I was hard for you even before then. I mean to ease my discomfort before getting back in the saddle."

"Can't someone else handle that for you? I get the impression your squires do more than clean your clothing."

"That's very perceptive of you. But I won't ask for that kind of service from them anymore. I am a simple man in many ways, and I have a code of conduct that I adhere to. One of those rules is that I take my marriage vows seriously. I will not seek my pleasure elsewhere now that we are wed."

"Huh! That makes you different than any other man I've known." Taryn was clearly not willing to believe him.

Soren forced the boy's chin up and ran his thumb over his pretty lips. "I am a Moorcondian prince. I would like to think that I *am* different than most men."

"And yet you have me kneeling before you like a supplicant."

"It is not intended to be demeaning, simply logistically beneficial."

Taryn's eyes flashed. "What does that mean?"

"It means I want your mouth."

"M-my mouth? There?" Taryn's gaze fixed on Soren's cock. His eyes had widened, so Soren couldn't miss the boy's blown pupils.

"That's right. I think you'll find it enjoyable. I know I will, and I'll gladly return the favor, if you want."

"No."

Soren wasn't sure what that one word was in response to, but he couldn't afford to waste more time finding out. Moving his hand to the back of Taryn's head, he gently pressed it forward and down to reach his cockhead. Taryn resisted only a little bit for a short time. It might have been his true desire emerging or simply due to his life-long experience that resistance was futile. In any event, Soren's higher brain functioning shorted out as soon as those luscious lips touched his dick.

When Taryn didn't open his mouth, Soren used his other hand to encourage his jaw to unhinge. The moment the lips parted a fraction, he fed his cock past them and into the wet heat of the boy's mouth. He had to suppress the groan, fearing that his men would hear too much of his pleasure. He didn't mind for himself but didn't want Taryn to feel more embarrassment than he already did. When the boy remained passive, he urged him to respond.

"Use your tongue to lave my shaft and suck as you do so. It will make me come faster," he added, hating to use a negative incentive, yet determined to work past his bride's resistance to him with whatever means possible.

And it worked. Taryn proved a quick study and a natural cocksucker. His velvety tongue worked the bundle of nerves underneath Soren's glans, and he began a rhythmic sucking that coaxed Soren's already-primed dick. He whipped his handkerchief from his sleeve to be the receptacle of his spending and pulled his cock out of Taryn's mouth at the onset of coming.

The force of it caused him to double over and he fisted his fingers in Taryn's hair. He grunted as the last of the cum spurted out and straightened.

Taryn stared back at him with his eyes still wide and his lips glistening with saliva. He wiped them on his sleeve and broke free of Soren's hold. Reluctantly, Soren allowed it. He stuffed his dick back into his trousers, aware that his erection hadn't fully abated. His desire for his bride wasn't easily satisfied, apparently. An apology rose within as he balled up his handkerchief and tossed it aside. The words stuck on his tongue and never came out because notwithstanding his bride's actions, the boy's cock was still stiff within his skirts.

Soren stood with a smile. "Let me ease your ache, my dear." He took a step forward.

Taryn took a step back. "No. It's nothing. I don't want you to touch me."

That assertion made Soren rather sad. "Please believe me when I say that your need is perfectly natural and nothing to be ashamed of." He took another step closer and tried to take hold of his bride once more.

Taryn ducked away with surprising speed and raced back to the convoy, and Soren could do little more than follow. By the time he caught up, Sam was already helping him back into the carriage. As much as Soren wanted to join his bride and press the issue, he knew that would be worse. The soldiers were watching him, knowing looks on their faces, but nothing malicious. As he'd told Taryn, they were happy for their prince and understanding that he was newly married. If he chased Taryn into the carriage, they'd know something was wrong, and that wasn't good for anyone.

Reluctantly, he plastered a cocky smile on his face and joined Rolf where the man held his horse's reins for him. He'd known him too long and trusted him too much to put up a front with him. He conveyed with his expression that he was both satisfied and frustrated, before swinging into the saddle.

"Let's go."

Chapter Three

"Would you like more water, your grace, or another slice of bread and cheese?"

Taryn shook his head while staring out of the window. "No, thank you. You have fed my hunger wonderfully, and I dare not drink more, not knowing when our next stop will be." That was mostly the truth, but disturbingly not the whole of it. He didn't want anything to wash away the lingering taste of Soren in his mouth. Or at least, he felt as if it were there. They had resumed their journey some time before, and he'd downed several cups of water. There really couldn't be any of Soren's tangy cum left. Still, he could conjure the memory of what little he'd experienced without any effort. And it felt as if the man's large cock remained sitting heavily on Taryn's tongue.

He should be furious over how his husband had insisted he suck his dick—and part of him was. But there was no denying that he'd also known a moment of disappointment when Soren had elected to come in a piece of cloth instead of inside Taryn's mouth. That brief taste of a few drops of cum had left him hungry for more. And his own dick pulsed at the thought of it. The book he'd placed on his lap when he'd first returned to the carriage remained fixed there. He couldn't bear the thought of Sam seeing him aroused. Did the squire know what had transpired out in those woods? Probably. All Soren's soldiers must, the lot of them being far more experienced than he about what could transpire between two men.

Hobart's incessant taunts rattled around in his head. *"Prissy little cocksucker. Why don't you put on a dress and service the longhouse guards? You know you want to."* Well, Taryn's brother was stupid about so many things, but in this, he'd proven to be prescient. Here Taryn sat, wearing a lovely gown and with the stark memory of sucking another man's dick fresh in his mind. He should feel worse about it than he did. Instead, he wondered if he might end up on his knees again before the day was out — the thought of it not repulsing him as it should.

"I'll gladly return the favor." Had Soren meant it? He'd seemed sincere. It was hard to picture the commanding prince kneeling between Taryn's legs and taking his cock into what must be a warm, snug place and sucking, and sucking... Taryn started, straightening from where he'd been resting his head against the side of the carriage. His cock and balls ached. He had to mash the book against his lap to get them under control.

"Are you all right, your grace?" Sam's eyes held no hint of teasing, only genuine concern. He'd put away the basket of food and was sewing the bodice of a green gown.

Taryn cleared his surprisingly tight throat. "Yes, thank you. I must have dozed off for a few seconds."

Sam smiled as he returned to his task. "That's easy to do. The journey is long and tedious, and the swaying of the carriage can put one to sleep quickly."

"Yes," Taryn agreed vaguely, not sure if had been the movement or the memories that had overwhelmed him so. Needing to change the subject of his own thoughts if nothing more, he asked a question he already knew the answer to simply to make conversation. "Is that another of the traveling dresses for me?"

"Yes, your grace. I altered a shift for you to sleep in tonight, and this will be done for tomorrow."

"You needn't put yourself to such bother. The shift I have on will serve me well enough tonight and with a little airing, this gown will be fine to wear again tomorrow."

Sam's eyes widened. "Oh no, your grace. It would be worth my hide if the dowager queen learned that I'd let you wear the same thing two days in a row."

His own disturbing and conflicting thoughts about Soren forgotten, Taryn leaned forward. "Would she really have you whipped?" The idea that his new in-laws were cruelly demanding didn't sit well with him. He'd somewhat hoped that he at least headed to a place not filled with fear as much as his father's domain.

Sam smiled. "No, your grace. I exaggerate. Although, believe me, you don't want to be on the other end of Queen Margrette's cutting tongue." The boy shook his head as he focused on a row of stitches. "The entire royal family is well-loved by Moorcondians. They are wise and just rulers." He snapped his thread with his teeth and peered with obvious judgment at his work. "Prince Soren in particular is revered by his men. To a man, if he told them to jump off a cliff, they would do so without hesitation, knowing that he would only give an order that was necessary for the greater good."

The squire held up the top half of the dress for Taryn to see. "There, your grace. I altered this the same as I did for the one you're wearing. I think the fit is good. Are you happy with it?"

It was on the tip of Taryn's tongue to say 'no' but that wouldn't be fair to the boy. He wasn't the one who had insisted on Taryn wearing a gown. "It's perfect, thank you."

Even as he said the words, Taryn wondered if he was truly expected to dress like a woman for the rest of his life or would everyone stop trying to pretend that he was Alissa. Despite Hobart's baiting, it wasn't the case that Taryn believed himself to be female. It was only that he was drawn to other men. Among the Marshers, that was a forbidden desire, no matter the reason why. Yet Soren and these other Moorcondians acted as if it were nothing of concern. Was that truly the case, that men lying with other men was acceptable, or did they too think Taryn was a woman born with the wrong anatomy?

Clearly pleased with Taryn's approval, Sam laid the dress on his lap and pulled out more thread. "Now, I need to redo the waist. I should have time before we stop for the night."

"When do you think that will be?" He hadn't lied to Soren when he'd said he was sore. No matter how much he shifted his weight, his hole ached as if Soren's cock were still embedded in it. That thought made his own dick perversely twitch with interest. He pushed the book down harder again and focused on listening to Sam's answer. It helped to distract him from his own traitorous body.

"Well before sundown, I should say. But the prince won't want to stop until we've met up with the others."

Taryn furrowed his brow. "What others?"

Now Sam looked flustered. "Oh, um, the rest of the prince's men. He, ah, left them nearby in case..."

"The offer of a treaty was a trap," Taryn finished, easing the boy's obvious embarrassment.

Sam ducked his head to concentrate on his work and to not look Taryn in the eye. "Yes, your grace. The prince is a brilliant tactician, always planning for all eventualities. He meant nothing by it, I'm sure, merely being cautious."

Taryn shifted his gaze to stare out of the window again. "As someone who has known my father my entire life, I can't fault the prince for his planning." He didn't trust the chieftain or Hobart, either, except for them to do whatever they thought was best for themselves. Even now, he wasn't sure if they meant to uphold the treaty. As essentially the hostage against the Marshers' good behavior, Taryn hoped so. He didn't want to imagine his fate if not. But worrying about his family's motives or next moves never did him any good, so he put the thoughts aside and let the carriage lull him to sleep once more.

* * * *

Taryn next woke when the carriage came to a stop. Sam had already packed away his sewing and leaned over to open the door next to Taryn. He didn't get a chance to do more than put his fingers on the handle before it flew open. Soren reached in a large hand in a silent command. Taryn chose not to make an issue out of it and told himself that it was courtesy and he should appreciate it as such—so he took it. As soon as his foot hit the raised step, Soren let go and grabbed Taryn's waist with both hands. The man swung him to the ground with ease. Compared to Soren's large proportions, Taryn was nearly as small and light as a child. The difference in their power, both politically and physically, should have made him uneasy. In some ways it did, but out here in places he'd never ventured before, it also made him feel safe.

"Thank you," he said, shaking out his skirts. It was weird how easily he'd adapted to this new mode of dressing so quickly. He took a step forward and swayed.

Soren clasped him by the shoulders to steady him. "Easy. Your body thinks it's still in the carriage. I'll walk you to where a rug is being laid for your comfort."

"I'm fine now, thank you." Taryn tried to push Soren away, but he may as well have tried to move a mountain for all the good it did him.

With his arm wrapped around Taryn's shoulders, Soren steered him through the throng of soldiers, horses and the various servants running to and fro to set up camp. Taryn could see that a large encampment was already laid out as far as his eyes could see. It was here, near a small lake, that Soren took him, so that by the time they reached their destination, he was cocooned within the army, well-guarded, although whether to keep him from leaving or being harmed was hard to tell. These new men were getting their first look at the prince's 'bride', and they weren't shy about their curiosity. Taryn made himself stand tall, knowing better than to show his discomfort and trepidation. Powerful men always took advantage of any weakness.

The waiting men greeted Soren respectfully but also with open affection. He, in turn, returned the salutations, calling out many by name. Taryn could see the truth in Sam's words about the loyalty these men had for their prince. By the time they arrived at a large rug spread out with pillows by the water's edge, Taryn's tension had eased. Everyone was too obviously happy for him to worry over much. The night would likely pass without incident — if one didn't count what Soren was going to do to him.

Taryn craned his neck around. "Where is your tent?"

"Still packed away. It takes too much time and effort to set it up only to tear it down again the next morning. We'll sleep here on the rug with blankets to ward off the chill of the night."

The pile of the carpet was lush, and the pillows at one end were large and fluffy. There were no covers to be seen, yet, but the other squire, Tom, was busy setting up a low table. "Will we eat here?" Taryn asked as Soren took him to the mound of pillows.

"Yes, the cook already set up here is likely nearly done preparing our dinner, given that I sent a man ahead to announce our imminent arrival." Soren paused and turned Taryn to peer into his eyes. "I left these men here just in case…diplomacy fell apart."

Taryn freed himself from the hold. "You needn't explain yourself to me. I understand what you did and why. Don't forget I know my father far better than you do." Sweeping his skirts aside in what was still an unfamiliar move, he sat with as much grace as he could. He was still holding his book, he realized and placed it back on his lap because his dick was trying to react to Soren's recent touch, no matter how much Taryn fought it. There was no way he wanted Soren's men to see his arousal. That thought led to another horrifying one — with no tent for privacy, was Soren going to fuck him out in the open for everyone to see and hear?

Soren planted his long legs in front of him. "I must go and confer with my sub-commanders. I'll be back to take my meal with you. Are you all right for now?"

Taryn glared up at him. "Of course. I couldn't be safer, surrounded by a thousand Moorcondian soldiers as I am."

Soren chuckled. "Not quite that many." He crouched down and spoke in a low tone. "These are your men, now, Taryn. You are my duchess, and they are loyal to you as that."

Because the man's gaze was so intense, Taryn had to look away. "If you say so."

On a sigh, Soren straightened and walked away. Taryn occupied his time by watching the goings-on around him. He had never been among so many men in his life. His father's warriors were plentiful but had paid him little attention, which had been all to the good. These Moorcondians appeared to be fierce fighters, but they were also clean, where the Marshers were a dirty and disheveled lot, more often than not. Everyone moved with efficient purpose, as well. No petty fights broke out among them. Taryn even spied women sprinkled among the larger group as Soren had mentioned. His father would never tolerate female warriors, no matter how big and skilled they were.

Sam appeared by his side with various pieces of cloth in hand. "Would you like to bathe after your long journey, your grace? There is plenty of hot water ready for you."

It was then that Taryn realized how dusty and sticky he felt. He stood. "That would be lovely, thanks. The lake will do well enough, however."

Sam looked aghast. "Oh, but, your grace, the water will be quite cold."

"That's all right. I prefer a brisk bath, given how fuzzy my head is from all of that napping." Taryn didn't wait for the squire's permission. He figured if he were truly a powerful duchess now, he could do as he liked, not what a servant wanted.

Sam confirmed his instincts by scurrying after him. By the water's edge, a row of men stood a few feet apart from each other, scanning the area. The squire overtook Taryn to approach a grizzled man who was built like a mountain.

"Sir Francis, the duchess wishes to bathe in the lake. Please take appropriate steps."

The soldier grimaced before shouting. "Turn around and eyes forward, lads. The duchess is in need of privacy."

Taryn stopped at the very edge of the water and slipped off his half-boots, then waited for Sam to tackle the laces in back. "Why do they feel the need to do that? We are all men, after all. What difference does it make if they see me?"

"You are the prince's consort. Your modesty matters. He wouldn't want any of his soldiers to see you naked."

Taryn rolled his eyes but said nothing more about it. It was almost comical how much everyone was determined to weave this fantasy that he was really a girl. But the water was so inviting that he put those thoughts aside and waded in as soon as he was stripped of his clothing. Thank the Gods his cock was mostly flaccid. The icy water ensured that it went completely limp. He was bracing to splash himself, and he longed for a quick swim, despite the coldness.

"Please, your grace, don't go too far."

Taryn glanced back at a worried Sam, who was undressing. "I'm a Marsher. I can swim almost as well as I can walk."

"I'm sure, your grace, but the prince —"

"Wouldn't like it. I understand." Taryn had to be satisfied with wading to his thighs and sluicing water on his upper body. He stood his ground, however, when a clearly uncomfortable Sam followed him with a bar of soap. "I'll wash myself, thank you. Go back to the bank." He made the order clear and firm, and the squire's obvious relief mollified Taryn's displeasure at his restrictions. At least he could have a positive impact on those beneath him.

The sun was dipping quickly, however, so he didn't linger. After a brief moment of indecision, he washed his hair as well. Once ashore, he let Sam rub him dry and pull a thick, opaque, white shift over his head. Then clean stockings and the half boots went on and finally a cloak was draped over his shoulders. He stood patiently while Sam wicked moisture from his hair, feeling refreshed and hungry.

"Would it be all right if I comb and braid your hair back on the rug, your grace?"

"Yes, I suppose that's fine." Long hair and braids on warriors were not unknown by his people, so he wasn't opposed to the idea on the principle that it made him look more like a woman. The squire's careful attention was quite soothing, actually, so that by the time Soren returned to his side, Taryn felt relaxed enough not to worry over the intrusion. The prince plopped down beside him, cross-legged. His hair was also wet, and he wore a casual tunic and trousers.

"I bathed the dust off me in the lake," the prince casually remarked. "I hear you did the same."

Of course, he had. Taryn doubted there was anything he could do that wouldn't be noticed and reported on. He lifted his chin. "Yes, I did. That's what the water is for. There was no need for anyone to go to the trouble of heating some. I don't need coddling. I'm not a girl, and even if I were, I'm a Marsher and used to making do with what nature provides."

"I meant no admonishment, my dear."

Taryn was pondering how he felt about the affectionate way Soren had taken to calling him when a heavy-set man strode over with two servants scurrying behind him. The man stopped short of stepping on the rug and bowed low. "Your highness, your grace." He straightened and gestured toward the boys, who kicked off their half-boots and stepped onto the rug. "I have roasted chicken and new potatoes with sautéed greens and mushrooms for your dining pleasure." He bowed again.

Sam moved the low table to a place right in front of Taryn and the prince before the other servants set two plates each on it. The smell was delicious, and Taryn's stomach rumbled at the anticipation of eating. Then he glanced around and saw the soldiers were gulping down food from bowls.

Confused, he asked, "Are we not having what everyone else is?"

The cook looked aghast for a second before banking his expression. "They are eating chicken stew with dumplings, your grace. Good enough for fighting men but not fit for a la...for a duchess." He bowed even lower this time, and Taryn worried that he would topple over.

Having honed a sense for mounting tension, Taryn fell back on his practice of defusing it. "It looks and smells wonderful. Thank you for your consideration."

The cook broke out into a smile, bowed once again then took his leave. Taryn didn't wait to start eating, even though he was aware that Soren hadn't begun. There was no admonishment for that breach of etiquette, and soon the prince picked up his fork, too.

"You will need to get used to others catering to you."

Taryn took a moment to savor the delicious piece of chicken he ate. For an army cook, the man was more skilled than any Taryn had known before. He swallowed it down with a sip of mead from a cup that Sam had silently placed on the table. "I am aware, and I *am* trying. I don't want to make trouble."

"With everyone but me."

Taryn stiffened at the rebuke, then glanced at his husband. The man wasn't mad. His expression was a teasing one. Taryn relaxed again. "Only in a certain way. And as it doesn't seem to matter to you how I feel about that..." He didn't finish, mindful that both the squires and servants hovered nearby and could hear every word, no matter how softly spoken.

"On the contrary, my dear. How you feel about that subject matters a great deal to me." He leaned into Taryn, close enough that his warm breath tickled Taryn's ear. "That's why I am determined to prove you wrong in your fears."

Taryn couldn't think of a proper response to that statement, so he didn't even try. Instead, he kept one hand lying in his lap as much as possible to hide how Soren's proximity and warm, inviting words affected him.

Dinner came and went quickly. There was some music played among the men as an after-dinner entertainment, but not for long. Quiet descended with the darkness of night and soon Taryn found himself lying against fluffy pillows with a soft blanket warding off the chilly air. It wasn't as effective, however, as the heat emanating off Soren's big body. The man had stripped down to his trousers before lying next to Taryn.

The fear of what was to come, laced with unwanted anticipation, made Taryn bold. "You aren't going to do anything to me, are you, where everyone can see and hear?"

Soren chuckled low and pulled Taryn against him. "Certainly not. I would never treat you with such contempt. I may not mind my men knowing that we have sex, but I don't want any of them to actually watch us. You'll be happy to know that until we reach home, this is how we will spend our nights—together yet chaste." Taryn relaxed at the news, then his heartbeat picked up at Soren's next words. "We'll have to be satisfied with stealing our pleasure during the breaks from our journey." He pressed a kiss against Taryn's temple before settling.

Taryn lay stiff in his husband's arms, determined not to find comfort there. Yet even with the slumber during the journey, he fell fast asleep.

* * * *

"We're approaching the city gates, your grace." Sam's head was practically turned all the way around as the squire looked out of the window at their approaching destination. "It will be good to see my family again. Mother was worried about my traveling into enemy territory." The import of his words must have registered, because the boy pulled his head back into the carriage with wide eyes. "I meant no offense, your grace."

Taryn hastened to reassure his traveling companion. Sam had been good company for the long journey. "I took none — and I know how you feel," he added under his breath. The tedium of his travels had caused him to wish for them to reach the end, but his stomach fluttered with nerves at the thought of entering the Moorcondian capital and the seat of their king's power. While he'd never been permitted to join in any war counsel discussions, he knew enough about how the world worked to understand that as a treaty bride, he was as much a hostage as a new member of the royal family. Being a Marsher, he wasn't certain what kind of treatment the court would give him.

Then there was the matter of his finally being bedded privately by the prince. Soren had made good on his promise not to take Taryn out in the open. That didn't mean there had been no sex. With each stop, Taryn had serviced his husband with his mouth. Each time, his husband had offered to return the favor, but he'd always refused. Much of it was him perversely sticking with his resistance to the marriage. But that wasn't the whole of it. Deep down, he knew that he would like it, and there were too many bad memories of his brother's endless baiting for him to give up the hard shell he'd erected around his own desires. This night, however, they would be alone once more, and his husband would want to claim as much as he had on the first occasion. The anticipation of it made him nervous and yet, he couldn't help thinking about it constantly. Not every thought when picturing the night to come was bad.

The carriage came to a sudden halt and horses legs pulled even with the window. "Sam, help the duchess alight." Just the sound of Soren's commanding voice set shivers skittering up Taryn's spine. He didn't resist when Sam did as he'd been told. Then there was Soren's hand, hovering down from where the man perched on his tall war horse. "Give the duchess a mounting block, boy."

Sam laced his fingers and held them out for Taryn to use as leverage. Taryn had never had trouble getting on a horse in his life, but he recognized that he wasn't going riding so much as joining Soren in the saddle. He felt an instinct to resist, but in the end did as he'd been commanded as he'd done his whole life. *It doesn't matter what I want. It never has.* He placed his hand in Soren's while putting his foot on Sam's and was pulled up to sit sideways in front of his husband. Feeling unsteady, he clutched at Soren.

The prince put one arm around Taryn's waist. "Not to fear, wife. I won't let you fall."

Taryn stared at the dirt road that led to tall gates that seemed to wrap around the mountain behind them. "Why do you want me here?"

"We are entering the city, and all will want a good look at the new Duchess of Vostguard."

That was all he said before kicking his horse into a canter. Taryn held on to the man's arm with a firmer grip, and at the same time, appreciated the wind being in his face and the race toward ending their days-long journey. The guards at the gate stood at attention as they passed and the throng of people lining the cobbled street inside the city parted for them as if moving at some unheard order.

There seemed to be thousands of people of all ages and classes, each one eagerly staring at their returning prince and his new bride. They should have been surprised to see a boy sitting on their prince's lap, yet their expressions didn't show any. Likely a herald had proceeded them with the news. If there was any resentment over Taryn's sex or his origin as a Marsher, there was no sign of it at all. Instead, there were loud cheers welcoming them home. He took in as much as he could of the gleaming city nestled in the mountains. It was extraordinary, and he'd never felt like such a dirty Marsher boy as he did then.

Except he was in the arms of a powerful Moorcondian prince and dressed in fine clothing. His hair was clean and held back in a single braid. There was nothing for him to feel ashamed about, and he wouldn't give anyone the satisfaction of seeing his insecurity. With his chin raised, he gave the masses as serene a look as he could manage. Near the end of the road stood an inner wall and another gate. They practically flew through them to enter the bailey of the palace. When they reached the wide, white steps leading to the imposing front doors of the building itself, Soren urged his horse to climb to the top, then turned around to face the crowd that had poured through behind them. The prince's hand slid up to grasp Taryn's braid. He turned Taryn's head and pulled it back before claiming his mouth with the kind of passionate kiss reserved for the bed chamber. Even louder cheers rose from the crowd, and by the time Soren let him up for air, Taryn was flushed, and his heart pounded.

Soren basked in the adulation of his people for a few more seconds before wheeling his horse around again to face the huge open double doors that led into the palace. An officious-looking man with short gray hair and clad in severe black clothing stood just outside them. He waited with hands clasped in front for Soren to first dismount, then help Taryn do the same. A sense of vertigo made him sway, but Soren's strong arm was there to steady him. They approached the man.

Soren spoke without preamble. "Minister Tost, I am pleased to present to you the new treaty with the Marsher Chieftain Hogard." Soren pulled folded thick sheets of paper from the inside of his tunic and presented them to the man with a flourish.

"Welcome home, your highness." The minister bowed low before accepting the papers. "The king has commanded me to commend you on your success. He asks that you seek him in his private quarters once you've seen the duchess settled." He looked at Taryn and bowed again. "Welcome to your new home, *Princess* Soren." There was, for the first time from any Moorcondian, a hint of derision.

Hearing himself referred to in such a way startled him more than being called a duchess had. Taryn got the feeling that the officious man used that title deliberately to emphasize that Taryn was viewed as being a woman in Moorcondia. He wasn't sure that was completely true, but he wasn't going to give the man the satisfaction of showing resentment. He had never held the notion that females were inherently inferior to males. And although he didn't intend to think of himself as a woman, there was also nothing demeaning about being one, either.

Soren stepped into the fray on his behalf, however, apparently understanding his feelings on the matter without having been told. "My wife prefers using the lessor title of Duchess of Vostguard. Please see that everyone at court understands that." There was an edge to the prince's tone, and for perhaps the first real time, Taryn appreciated having such a powerful ally.

The minister nodded. "Certainly, your highness."

Without another word, Soren breezed past the man and the guards flanking the doors as if he owned the palace — and he kind of did. His family had ruled

Moorcondia for many generations. Taryn tried not to gawk too much as he was briskly escorted through the elaborate seat of Soren's family's power. Everything was so big and shiny that it was like walking through an opulent dream of a place that could only be lived in by the gods. And each person they passed bowed or curtsied, decked in finery surpassing what Taryn himself had been given to wear. Even liveried servants wore nicer clothing than a Marsher chieftain. Soren often called out to them by name, and it didn't take any imagination to see how well regarded, if not loved, he was by his people.

They went up a flight of stairs, then down a long hall, before turning off into a wide wing of the palace. There were so many twists and turns that Taryn feared he would get forever lost if no one was there to guide him. Finally, they stopped in front of a heavy-looking carved door. Soren opened it and brought Taryn into a beautiful sitting room, decorated in fine fabrics in cheery and very feminine colors and prints.

"This is your sitting room," Soren said as he navigated the furniture toward another door.

"Mine?" Taryn couldn't keep the surprise from his voice. If he'd had a chance to consider it, he might have thought it belonged to the dowager queen.

"Yes. You may change it however you wish to suit your tastes."

Taryn became more overwhelmed with his surroundings at the pronouncement that he was now to make decisions about decorating, of all things. Then they passed through the far doorway and his attention was captured by a bedroom done in similar taste, with a large canopy bed and a fireplace to match the one on the other side of the wall. If nothing else, he would never again be cold at night.

Soren stopped in the middle of the room. His grip tightened. "And this is your bedroom…obviously. You may likewise order whatever new furniture and fabrics as you please."

The tenseness of Soren's tone was not lost on Taryn. He'd come to be able to read the man quite well in the few days they'd known each other. The cause of the stress dawned on him with only a moment's thought. "This was your first wife's room?"

Soren's jaw twitched. "It is for my duchess," he allowed before tugging Taryn once more over to a smaller door that led into a passageway. "This is the garderobe and bathing facilities. It connects our two bedrooms."

"Oh." Taryn had been processing the marvel of internal plumbing when his mind focused on that last bit. "Do we need that?"

Soren looked at him with a familiar heat in his eyes. "It will allow me to visit you at night in privacy."

Taryn felt his cheeks heat. "I suppose you'll want to do that often."

Before Soren could give the obvious answer, their attention was caught by a chorus of female voices. "Papa, are you here?"

Soren's face broke out into a wide smile, and he hurried Taryn through the connecting tunnel into his room. It was a masculine mirror of what was now Taryn's, as was the sitting room that really served as an office with a large, polished dark-wood desk. Taryn had only a moment to take it all in before he was surrounded by four girls of various ages, pretty as peacocks and each one with a head of dark red hair. A plain, older woman trailed after them with a frown on her face.

"Papa!" The youngest of them, a girl of perhaps ten, launched herself into Soren's arms.

He twirled her around before setting her on her feet again and peppering her with kisses on her head. The other three crowded him on all sides and were treated to a similar show of affection. The unguarded moment eased some of the tension inside Taryn. Soldiers and servants could fake adoration, but children were a good test of a man's character. These girls were clearly delighted to see him.

"Did you miss us, Papa?" the youngest asked.

Soren tapped the tip of her nose with his forefinger. "Terribly. But I said I'd be back in no time at all, and I was right, wasn't I? Hardly two weeks have passed."

"That's true," the child allowed. Then she turned her bright green eyes on Taryn and looked at him with an assessing eye. "How come our new mother is a boy?"

The oldest girl, perhaps a few years younger than Taryn, gasped and gave her sister's braid a good yank. "Lilli! I told you not to ask questions."

The girl glared at her older sister. "But, Nora, I don't want to be the youngest anymore. Papa said I'd get a baby brother or sister." She looked up at Soren. "Papa, can a boy mother give me that?"

The older woman muttered something about the gods preserving them all and shook her head. Soren, however, laughed and smoothed the hair on his daughter's head. "I'm afraid not, Lillibet. There has been a change in plans. This is Taryn. He has become my wife."

The prince looked at him, and there was a softness to his gaze that Taryn hadn't seen before. "These are my daughters. Eleanora, Duchess of Windham and Countess of Kenworth... She is my heir and chatelaine for my estates. These are my fearsome twins, Margrette and Vivienne. Although they were born minutes apart, they are like chalk and cheese. Thank the gods they aren't identical or there would be no end of mischief." He smiled, and the twins smiled back, this obviously being a running joke between them. He patted the youngest on her head. "And this imp is Lillibet."

All four girls curtsied to him with flawless grace, although he rather suspected that, being princesses, they were of higher rank than he was. Should he bow to them in return…or curtsy? He wasn't sure what to do, given that he wore a dress. In the end, he bowed his head. "I am pleased to meet you." Then he waited to see how they would receive him. The littlest had already broached the main issue.

Margrette cocked her head as she looked at him, giving him a curious look. She was just on the cusp of womanhood and her stare unnerved him. "How is it supposed to work, then, two men being married? Is that even possible?" she asked her older sister.

Vivienne elbowed her in the ribs before Eleanora could muster a reply. "Don't be rude."

"I'm only asking the obvious question. I mean, unlike *some*, I know that a boy can't have a baby, but honestly how is it that they —?" The girl grunted when her twin stomped on her foot.

"I'll explain it later," Vivienne said in a low voice that nevertheless was heard by all.

Taryn figured his cheeks were on fire because his embarrassment was so keen, and he looked at Soren for guidance. The man had the audacity to be chuckling silently over his daughter's questions.

The governess was not so amused. She clapped her hands. "Now then, princesses, that's enough. Your father undoubtedly has important business to attend to with the king, and the duchess needs rest from her…ah, *the* long journey."

Eleanora nodded. "Quite right, Dame Agnes. Lessons for the day are not over."

Margrette frowned. "Easy for you to say… You don't have to do them. They're so boring." She rolled her eyes.

Her older sister was not having any of it. "If you want to trade places with me, feel free. The ledgers from Kenworth have newly arrived and sit on my desk waiting for review. Have at it, and I'll do whatever you have left for the day."

Margrette huffed. "Geography. I hate it."

"I love it," Vivienne chimed in, which earned her a deeper frown from her sister.

Dame Agnes made a shooing motion. "Come on, your highnesses. *Out*."

The three younger girls left, dragging their feet, but the oldest remained. "Papa, when you have time, there is a matter I wish to discuss with you."

"I must go to the king, as Dame Agnes surmised, then there is the banquet. Can it wait until tomorrow?"

"Of course, but if you are speaking with the king…an offer was made for me while you were away."

Soren's expression turned thunderous in the blink of an eye. "Who?"

"Lord Beasley."

"That weasel. He waited until I was gone to make his move."

Eleanora put a calming hand on her father's arm. "The king turned him down."

"As well he should have."

"I believe it was mostly because I won't be of marriageable age for another year. At least, that is what I heard. No one has said anything to me directly about it. I was hoping you might entreat the king on my behalf for some say in any future offers."

Soren cupped his daughter's face with his hands. "I will make sure that whoever you marry, it is someone you want."

"Thank you, Papa, but I don't expect you to make a promise you cannot keep." She glanced at Taryn. "You had little say in your own future in that regard, after all."

Soren sighed and dropped his hands. "You have always been too clever by half—just like your mother."

The girl grinned. "So you have said before, and I take that as a compliment."

"Good, because it was meant as one. I will speak with the king. Beasley will not have you. That is a promise I can most definitely keep."

"Thank you, Papa." She turned to Taryn. "Welcome to the family, your grace." She curtsied again.

Taryn bowed his head. "Thank you, your highness."

She smiled. "Call me Nora. Everyone in the family does."

And just like that, Taryn suddenly felt that he had indeed found his new home. How he was going to fit in was another story altogether.

Chapter Four

Soren watched as his bride moved around the sitting room, peering at each piece of furniture and accent piece. The awe and appreciation in the boy's expression was delightful to see. It helped dull the ache lodged in Soren's chest over being in Merida's private space, something he'd avoided since her death.

Taryn ran his fingers along the back of one chair. "This is silk, is it not?"

Somewhat surprised that a Marsher would recognize the fabric, Soren said, "Yes."

A wistful look crossed his bride's face. "My mother bought a piece of it off a tinker once. She used half of it for a burial shroud for my grandmother. She had wanted to use the rest for her own, but my father sold it."

Asshole! The more he heard about Hogard, the happier he was to have taken Taryn away from the fucker's control. "As I said, you can redecorate this however you want. Silk is plentiful here."

Taryn looked over at him. "But no less expensive, I should wonder. It would be wasteful to change what is already so beautiful."

"My dear, I realize we haven't had much chance to talk. I am a very wealthy man, and what is mine is now yours. You could redo this room a hundred times, using the best materials, and it would barely make a dent in my coffers."

Taryn moved on to gaze at the various pretty objects sitting on a shelf. "I assumed you were rich, given that you are a Moorcondian prince. I would not presume, however, to have the right to spend your money as I wish."

Soren's new duchess really was a sweet, little thing. Using endearments with him tripped naturally off his tongue. Now that he was home, it was getting even easier to accept the fact that he was married to another male, surprisingly so. Perhaps the way things had worked out was a blessing. Having another woman rummage through Merida's possessions would have been harder, now that he thought about it.

"Presume away. My daughters certainly do. All except Eleanora," he amended. "She has her own substantial wealth."

Taryn paused and pursed his lips. "Why does she have titles other than princess?"

"Windham is the duchy she inherited from her mother. Kenworth is my lessor title and given as a courtesy to the heir."

"I see. Everything is so complicated here. In the Marshlands, there is a chief, then everyone else. Even my older brother has no title of his own."

Soren scratched at the back of his neck. "I hadn't thought of my people in those terms, but we do have a complex hierarchy, now that you mention it. I suppose it takes an outsider to highlight the things we take for granted."

Taryn moved to run his fingers along the heavy drapes. "This material is so soft. I think I saw people dressed in it on our journey through the palace."

"Indeed. It is velvet, very popular for clothing."

Taryn turned to look at him once more. "Is it hard for you to be here? In this room, I mean."

The question stunned Soren for a moment. His new wife was surprisingly perceptive…and compassionate, given his expression. Soren considered brushing it off, then the truth came tumbling out anyway. "Yes, actually." He stared at his own toes for a moment. "I haven't been in here since she died."

"How long ago was that?"

"Nearly five years." The pain of it stabbed him fresh, although not quite as sharp as it once had been. "Merida died the spring after both my parents succumbed to the avian plague."

"Oh." Taryn looked away and blinked hard a few times. "I'm sorry. I lost my mother to that, as well."

Soren did the math. "You must have been very young." He almost dreaded the answer, having not had time to consider how old his bride was. Moorcondian law said one must be at least sixteen to wed, although few actually did so at that tender age. What was the Marsher custom?

Taryn shrugged. "About the same age as the twins. Not so young." That caused Soren to breathe an inner sight of relief. That would make Taryn eighteen — younger than Soren would like, yet not a child by his own society's standards.

Taryn furrowed his brow. "I hadn't realized your parents are dead. I thought when Sam said the dowager queen had sent my trousseau, he'd meant…"

"That was my grandmother, Dowager Queen Margrette."

"How sad for her to see her child die before her."

"She is a formidable woman. You'll meet her soon, although probably not at tonight's banquet. She hates those kinds of affairs."

Alarm crossed Taryn's face. "I'm going to be presented to the king tonight? I had thought perhaps after a few days."

Soren tried to give him a reassuring smile. "Not to worry. He doesn't bite—nor does his queen. They do, however, want to meet you and introduce you formally to the court. Best to get it over with, don't you think?"

"I suppose." Taryn bit his lower lip. "Do you think everyone is going to accept your bride being a boy?"

Not wanting to start his marriage with lies, Soren was frank. "Most will, simply because it doesn't matter to them. Some may not for their own provincial reasons. They won't dare to show their feelings on it, though. The king is going to present you as my duchess, and if the king wills it, it shall be so. You must tell me if anyone disrespects you," he added, suddenly protective of this vulnerable boy he'd brought home with him.

"I don't want to cause trouble."

Soren closed the gap between them and cupped Taryn's chin. He didn't miss how the boy nearly tried to avoid his touch, nor how he relaxed into it almost immediately. "You would *not* be causing trouble. Anyone who insults you insults me. And anyone who insults me insults the crown. That will not be tolerated." He peered closely into Taryn's eyes. Such a lovely shade of light green. He hadn't known Marshers could have such coloring. He'd only seen mud-brown in his interactions with them. "Do you understand?"

Taryn nodded, then backed away from Soren's touch in a smooth move that somehow didn't leave Soren feeling slighted. "I don't know what to wear!"

"Ah." In this, he could be reassuring. "Any time now, someone will arrive who will sort that all out for you." He heard a brisk knock a moment later and called out. "Come in."

The door opened and Rolf strode through, still dusty from their journey. Behind him came the pretty and elegant boy Soren had remembered. He was dressed immaculately in livery, yet managed to give it some flair of his own. Plus, he seemed to be wearing a bit of color on his lips and cheeks. *Perfect.*

Rolf bowed at Taryn. "Your grace, may I present my cousin, Kexen. He is keen to act as your maid, if you will have him."

Kexen gave Soren and Taryn a courtly bow with perfect form and more of that flair. "Your highness, your grace, I am honored at the privilege."

Taryn frowned. "My maid?"

Rolf gave Soren a look that clearly said he was not going to respond to that remark. Soren shrugged. "Yes, well, valet doesn't seem quite right."

"A maid implies a woman. Are you a woman?" Taryn directed his question to Kexen.

The page didn't answer right away. "I'm not *not* a woman, your grace." Everyone was still processing that odd response when the boy added, "Might I suggest we refer to me as your personal groomer? There will be maids to clean your chambers, but I will see to your bathing, clothes and hair — if you'll have me, of course, your grace." He gave another bow and grinned broadly. At least someone was happy about the situation.

Kexen's openness seemed to put Taryn at ease. "I think that's an excellent solution. And there is a banquet tonight, so I need something other than the traveling gowns Queen Margrette was kind enough to send me."

"Oh, the banquet, yes. I've seen them setting the grand dining hall for it. It's going to be amazing. And I've got some ideas already of what you should wear." The boy was practically bouncing on his feet. "Again, if it pleases you, your grace."

Taryn smiled. "Yes, thank you."

Kexen softly clapped his hands. "No, thank *you*, your grace. Let's get you into a nice, warm bath. You must be desperate for one after that long journey."

"I could use one," Taryn allowed. "But if everyone is busy, I don't want to bother the maids to bring up hot water."

Kexen glanced at Rolf before saying, "Oh, but there's no need. I only have to turn on the tap. The palace has wonderful plumbing and provides a continuous flow of hot water to every bathing room."

Taryn blinked a few times. "Oh."

"This way, your grace." Kexen somehow managed to herd Taryn into the bedroom without touching him.

The last Soren saw of his bride was the boy glancing over his shoulder with a perplexed expression. Soren gave him a reassuring smile, then turned to Rolf.

"Well, that's one thing that's gone to plan."

"I'd say so, your highness."

"What was all that about not *not* being a woman?"

"I can't say exactly. But the boy has always loved wearing his sister's gowns, and he does look quite lovely in them, too. And I'm sure you noticed the face paint, another thing he favors, as well as styling his hair in elaborate fashion when not on duty. At the same time, he's wicked with a fencing blade, has a seat that rivals the best cavalrymen and manages to take down larger men than he without breaking much of a sweat. We in the family have long ago accepted him as he is — a sweet and strong person with one foot in each camp, if you will. If anyone in this realm can figure out a way for your duchess to dress that satisfies all concerned, it's him."

"Good. That's one less thing for me to worry about." He grimaced. "I must hurry to the king. I've tarried too long, and you know that his majesty doesn't like being kept waiting."

Rolf followed him into the hall. "I'm sorry it took me a while to locate Kexen. I found him in an alcove in an intimate position with Lord Fenley, dirty old goat."

That news cheered Soren even more. "Perhaps he can guide my bride in that regard as well, then. Kexen...not Lord Fenley."

Rolf grinned. "I believe the duchess and Kexen will become great confidants."

"Good," Soren said again. "Taryn will need all the friends he can get in this strange new home of his."

Rolf peeled off at the next hallway, while Soren continued to the king's chambers. He heard his name being called. Stopping, he saw a small group of women coming his way. His heart sank a little when he realized who was leading the pack.

"Lady Balter." He nodded briefly at the stately woman, made taller by her elaborate coiffeur.

She curtsied deeply, those locks — and her bosom — bobbing as she did. When she straightened again, she gave him a look that he knew well to mean she was eager to get him alone. "Welcome home, Prince Soren," she said in a low voice that hovered between a purr and a growl.

"Thank you. I'm happy to be back."

"And successful as well — although from what I hear, not in the expected way."

Soren strove for patience. His unusual marriage was going to be a topic of conversation for some time. "The Marsher chieftain did substitute one child for another under unforeseen circumstances."

"A boy," the lady said in a tone that implied she was revealing a terrible secret. As if Soren hadn't noticed already that his bride had a cock.

"Yes," he simply said, clasping his hands tightly behind his back in order to hide how irritated he was.

Balter licked her lips just the way she did before taking his dick into her mouth. Funny how that gesture normally made him hard. Not this time. He found it contrived now. "Then our arrangement need not change, given that you're not really married again."

Soren had ended their affair before leaving because of his strong belief in being faithful to his vows and his wife. He couldn't understand why she thought Taryn's sex made a difference and let his perplexity show. "Yes, madam, I am. The marriage is legally binding in both countries. That's why it sealed the treaty," he added, knowing that the woman cared nothing for politics outside the jostling inside the palace.

The woman pouted. "Yes, yes — *legally*. But not in your heart. Surely you don't want the dirty Marsher boy."

Soren's patience snapped. He leaned into his former lover and let her see his displeasure. "Do *not* speak disrespectfully about my duchess. Taryn is a lovely boy, and I like him very much." He pulled back and plastered a smile on his face for the benefit of the ladies hovering in the background, eagerly watching and listening. "You'll get to meet him tonight. I trust you will all give him a warm welcome." He let the subtle threat hang in the air.

"Certainly, your highness." Balter and her coterie all curtsied as they simpered over how eager they were to make the new duchess's acquaintance.

"Excellent. Now if you'll excuse me, I don't want to keep the king waiting."

With that, he continued on his way, happy to enter his brother's private hall to get away from more prying eyes of the court. Here, there was quiet. No one entered unless invited to. The only people he encountered were the many guards lining the route to the king's suite. He knew each of them by name and was certain that they would lay down their lives for his brother. As a ruler, his brother, like their father before him, had worked to gain the admiration and trust of the soldiers he relied on. It wasn't enough to be born king. One's fate rested with the will of the people and no more so than with those who could skewer your heart without warning.

The guards flanking the doors to the king's reception room bowed at his approach and one of them opened the doors to announce his arrival. "His most royal highness, Prince Soren, Duke of Vostguard."

Soren kept a smile off his lips as he stepped into the room. The pomp and ceremony that colored his life was silly at its core, yet critical to maintain the power of the king. There was nothing Soren wouldn't put up with to support his brother. His recent marriage was a case in point.

He approached the wide chair that the king occupied, surrounded by various courtiers and guards, with his usual afternoon mug of beer in one hand. Soren bowed low. "Your majesty." He grunted as his brother enveloped him in a hug, sloshing beer on his shoulder. He returned the gesture. "I haven't been gone that long."

Auden returned to his chair and grinned. "It wasn't the length of your departure but the reason for it. When the heralds arrived to announce your success and imminent return, I breathed freely for the first time since you'd left."

"I must confess to a similar reaction when I crossed our borders. The journey was not without its moments of tension and uncertainty."

Auden motioned for him to take his usual nearby seat. "I understand there was a dramatic turn of events, marriage-wise."

Soren accepted the mug of beer brought by a servant and took a long pull of it before answering. "Yes. Apparently the chieftain's daughter preferred a life of celibacy and quiet contemplation over the horror of becoming my duchess."

Auden chuckled. "I'm sure she grew up on tales of Moorcondians drinking the blood of virgins. Good for her to take her fate into her own hands," he added, draining his own mug and holding it out for refilling.

"It was an admirably bold move, to be sure, but one that almost destroyed the treaty."

"Good thing Hogard had a substitute at hand."

"Yes. Taryn."

Auden's eyes twinkled. "I hear he's very pretty."

"Indeed. In that, I was fortunate. He looks nothing like a typical Marsher boy."

"Lucky for you." Auden drank some more. "Is he happy with the arrangement?"

"Not entirely." But Soren was determined to change that, although he wasn't going to get into those kinds of details with so many ears listening.

"A pity. We all must do our duty, however. He'll adjust in time. Although…it's a bit of a tangle, isn't it? Hard to know the best way to incorporate a male bride into court life." He turned to Tost, who hovered nearby, as always. Soren wasn't fond of the man, but he was an excellent minister and loyal to Auden, so that was all that mattered. "Is there any precedence for this, Tost?"

The minister came closer. "None, your majesty, although I can confirm that it is legal, so long as it was consummated," he added, eyeing Soren with an unspoken question hanging in the air.

"It was." He couldn't help being curt with the man. "I know the treaty laws, Lord Minister. My squires can testify to the consummation, should it become necessary."

"Not at all," Tost seemingly hastened to smooth over Soren's ruffled feathers. "I merely needed to confirm the obvious truth for purposes of the records of royal marriages."

Auden huffed. "I'm sure you did, Tost." To Soren, he added, "And you like fucking pretty boys as much as you do women, so no hardship for you, eh, brother?"

"None, your majesty." He kept his tone formal with no hint of his true feelings on the subject, nor the way in which his body was reacting to the topic."

Auden handed his mug to a nearby servant. "Everyone out. I would speak with my brother in private."

The room cleared within seconds as Auden's affable manner didn't fool anyone. He brooked no disobedience. All that remained were the guards stationed around for the king's protection, and they were deaf to everything said in that room. Soren relaxed into his chair because he knew he spoke only with his brother, not the king.

Auden leaned forward, elbows resting on his thighs. "How is it, really?"

Soren gave him the brutal truth, because this was the only person alive with whom he could truly do so. "I almost feel like I could be a rapist in my own marriage."

Auden winced. "I am sorry to hear that, brother, although not surprised. These political marriages are never about free choice. You and I and our parents were the exceptions, finding love where the good of the country dictated our futures. I'm sorry to have had to add insult to the injury of your losing Merida."

Soren waved away the apology because he knew that the treaty was essential to the wellbeing of their people. If Auden hadn't forced the issue, he would have insisted on cementing the treaty with his body himself. "It is not such a hardship. Other than his resistance to the marriage bed, Taryn is a nice boy. The girls seem to like him."

"High praise indeed. And if he can navigate his way through those four forces of nature, he is well-deserving of admiration." They traded an amused smile before he turned serious again. "Does he despise the touch of another man that much?"

Soren pictured his bride's expressions in unguarded moments. "Actually, I think he likes it well enough but can't allow himself to enjoy it. He keeps saying how unnatural it is, and we know how prudish the Marshers can be. It's likely that his inclinations in that regard were noticed and beaten out of him — literally — by his brutish father and brother. With patience, I hope to break down those barriers."

Auden rose and went to the sideboard where the pitcher of ale and his mug stood. After pouring himself more beer, he brought the pitcher over to top off Soren's. "Is Hogard as bad as all of the reports have said?"

Soren grimaced. "Worse."

"Ouch." The king sat again, putting the now-empty serving container on the floor, not bothering to return it to the sideboard. Some page would fetch it soon enough. "If nothing else, you've taken the boy away from all that misery. I know you can give him a good life here, better than any he could have ever hoped for. He'll come around."

"I hope so, but I don't want him giving himself to me out of gratitude. I need to show him how good it can be between us. Then we can build a life together that will at least have passion, if not love." As he said those words, however, some part of his mind chided him for setting his goals so low. Taryn was someone who could be loved. That much was certain.

"Well, let's also hope that Hogard upholds the treaty."

"He should. His people will greatly benefit from what we can give them. It won't be as much as their raids produce, but it will not come at the cost of spilled blood and spent resources on their end, either. It should be a win for him."

Auden, as was his wont, got to the heart of the matter. "You don't think he'll honor it, do you?"

Now it was Soren's turn to rise. He paced around the sitting area. "Fuck me, I don't. Having met the man, he does not strike me as the rational type. He wears his feelings on his sleeve, and there was nothing but contempt there for me, the wedding and the piece of paper he scratched his illegible name on."

"Surely, he understands that his son is as much a hostage as a pampered bride."

Soren stopped short, pain stabbing his chest. This was one aspect of his marriage that he had refused to face until now. "He doesn't care. I'm certain of it."

Auden peered into his mug. "A pity, then. Taryn is your wife, however, so I will leave matters entirely up to you…should the need arise."

Relief flooded him with sufficient force to catch him off-guard. He threw himself into his chair and gulped down the rest of his beer, trying not to dwell on how his brother's pronouncement had affected him. Besides, there was more to discuss than the Marshers.

"Speaking of marriage, I heard that Beasley made an offer for Nora."

Auden laughed. "Oh yes, he did, the twit. I turned him down…naturally."

"*Naturally.*" Fresh off his own political union, Soren couldn't be as sanguine, however. "He will try again."

Auden gave him his '*don't be stupid*' look. "Of course, he will. He thought to jump the line a year before her maturity. Others will be doing the same as she approaches her next birthday, men far better than Beasley. He's a fool to think he could control that wealth based on marriage alone. He obviously doesn't know our Nora as he should. She will not yield her authority to a husband in order to pursue needlework and gossip.

"As the holder of the lands of both Vostguard and Windham, she is a prize above virtually all others. We will not give her away so easily." Soren leaned toward his brother. It was critical that he be heard on this, the king's power be damned. "She is not a *prize*. She is my daughter. I would see her happy, brother. And I don't want her wed at sixteen simply because the law allows it. She deserves a few more years of freedom, as much as her station permits."

Auden's expression turned stern. "I love her too, Soren. I want her to be happy, but I also must do what's best for Moorcondia. There is no rush to marry her off, and I promise that both you and she will have a say in her future. More so than you had," he added, downing the rest of his beer.

"Thank you, brother." Soren knew when to back off. He'd gained enough concessions on the matter for the time being.

"And it won't be Beasley," the king added.

"Once again, thank you." Soren sighed. "I should see how the men are faring after the journey and get a bit of practice in after so many days in the saddle. I need to work off some energy before the tedium of the banquet."

"We are of a mind there, brother. Your bride must be officially introduced to the court, however, so best to get it out of the way quickly. Then we can get on with our lives."

Soren understood the need to adhere to protocol, but once that was done, he would be facing the night with his bride. They would be bedding down alone for the first time in days. His cock stirred at what that meant. He could only hope Taryn wasn't dreading that as much as the banquet. Even as he thought it, however, he knew his hopes would be dashed.

* * * *

"Did you have a nice rest, your grace?"

Taryn pushed up to a sitting position and watched Kexen as he lay a bundle of clothing gently down on a big chair by the fireplace. "Yes, thank you. I seem to be sleeping a lot since becoming a duchess." He wasn't used to having so much free time. The idea that he could simply lie down whenever he wanted was a strange one to him.

Kexen chuckled. "Get used to it, your grace. It is the life of a privileged woman."

Taryn sighed. "It seems decadent."

"And so it is." Kexen turned to him. "Can I get you anything?"

"No, thank you." Taryn pushed the covers aside and slipped out of bed. Kexen had found a man's nightshirt so that he didn't have to wear a woman's shift all the time. It made him feel more like himself. "What do you have there?"

Kexen's eyes lit up. "Your clothing for the banquet. If you agree, that is."

Taryn got closer. "Show me." He could already see beautiful colors of blue and silver.

Kexen held up the first of the items — a shiny, blue, sleeveless gown woven with threads of silver. The pattern was intricate, and as he reached it, he could see that it was some kind of flower motif he didn't recognize. "It's beautiful." He touched the fabric. "Is this silk?"

Kexen nodded. "Silk brocade. The head seamstress found it for me in an old cupboard filled with clothing from my grandmother's era. See how the neckline is high and V shaped? That was the style back then, more modest. Wearing this instead of the current styles won't emphasize how you don't have...um, a décolletage," the boy finished delicately.

Taryn felt his cheeks heat, and he nearly touched his chest. His lack of breasts was the most obvious sign that he wasn't the woman people expected him to be. "Yes, I can see the benefit of that." He stood back a bit to study the rest of the dress. It fell to floor-length, fitting his size and not needing any hemming. Or, perhaps Kexen had seen to that already.

"And see here, your grace." Kexen held the skirt out. "There are slits up to your hips. This kirtle would normally be worn over an underdress with long sleeves and in a complimentary color. As the woman would walk, flashes of the underskirt would show. I'm sure it was considered quite daring in its time."

Kexen lay the gown over the back of the chair before picking up two other items. "Instead of an underdress, I thought you could wear this dove-gray silk shirt with sleeves laced up the arm in dark blue thread. It's something a man would have worn under a short tunic. These tight-fitting trousers will show through the slits, giving the same effect as it would with a woman, yet with entirely masculine attire."

Taryn touched the trousers, as well. They were such a dark blue to be almost black and the fabric was the same soft material as the curtains in the sitting room. "This is velvet?"

"Yes, your grace. It goes very well with silk, and the darker blue compliments the lighter shade in the kirtle. Oh." He turned to the chair once more. "I found these boots in the same shade as the shirt to bring the whole ensemble together." They were just high enough to cover the ends of the trousers and looked softer than anything he'd worn to date, more like dainty slippers, yet also sufficiently masculine. "What do you think, your grace?"

Kexen looked at him with such hope that Taryn would have said anything to make him happy. As it was, he could tell his groomer the truth. "It's brilliant. All of it. Thank you, Kexen."

The boy sketched a bow. "It is my pleasure, your grace." He put everything back on the chair and stood admiring it all for a few seconds.

A thought occurred to Taryn, something that had been brewing since Kexen had been brought to him. "You love clothes, don't you?" When his groomer nodded with a smile, Taryn pushed it further. "Do you...ever wear stuff like this yourself? Like, ah, dresses? Not that it's any of my business," he added hastily, because it wasn't. Curiosity had gotten the better of him, though. Kexen might be dressed in the livery of a palace page, but his blond hair was braided in a pretty style down his back and there was definitely an artificial tinge to his lips and cheeks.

Kexen beamed at him. "You may ask any question about me you like, your grace. I don't mind. And the answer is yes, I do like wearing dresses sometimes." He shrugged. "I like variety and don't see why I have to limit my wardrobe to conventional items." His mouth formed a thin line, giving him a more serious expression than he'd worn to date. "I also don't understand why I have to be just one gender all the time. Can't I be both...or neither?"

The question startled Taryn. He'd never heard anyone express the idea before, had never considered it himself. As he had no answer in any event, he decided to take it as rhetorical. "I guess you are the perfect choice, then, in being the one to dress a boy bride."

Kexen's face lit up, banishing the stern one. "I believe that was the prince's very thought when he told my cousin, Rolf, to fetch me for the job."

Huh. With everything so new and overwhelming, Taryn hadn't considered how Kexen had ended up with the job of navigating the thorn bush that was Taryn's new clothing life. It was sweet that Soren had bothered and had found the perfect solution. Nothing required his new husband to care at all about what would please Taryn, so the man deserved credit where it was due.

"I suppose we should get me ready for the banquet." He palmed his stomach in reaction to the nervous fluttering inside it.

"Yes, your grace. Let's get you washed up from your nap, and I'll do your hair once you're dressed. Tonight won't be as bad as you think, if I may say so."

Taryn gave the boy a wan smile. "It's probably not possible for it to be. My imagination runs wild, I must confess. Will you be there?"

Kexen giggled. "I'm afraid not, your grace. I might have been if I were still merely a page in order to wait on tables. As your personal groomer, my duty is to be here when you return and ready you for retiring."

"Oh, yes, of course." Because any talk of the night to come made him think of what Soren intended to do to him in bed, he turned his thoughts from it.

He gave himself over to Kexen's care, allowing his groomer to freshen him up, slip the clothing over him, then sit him down in front of a delicate vanity with a tall mirror. It was hard to believe he was looking at himself. The clothing he wore was a perfect fit and transformed him from a dirty Marsher boy into some kind of exotic being.

"For your hair, I thought to make a braid at each temple. This much," Kexen added, taking hanks of hair in both hands. "Soldiers in the old days used to do much the same before going into battle, so it's nothing like how I've done mine or the even more elaborate coiffeurs of the court ladies."

"That sounds fine, then." Taryn sat still while Kexen's nimble fingers formed delicate braids woven with silver thread on each side of his head. Then he tied them together with a silver ribbon that he pulled from his pocket.

Kexen grinned at him from behind. "What do you think, your grace?"

Taryn turned his head one way, then the other. "It's…"

"Beautiful." Soren's image appeared in the mirror. He was imposing and magnificent in a tunic and trousers of plain dark blue and black boots up to his knees. A heavy belt holding a sword wrapped around his waist. His hair was pulled straight back, displaying his handsome face.

Kexen moved away to allow Taryn to stand, giving the prince an unobstructed view of his bride. The look in Soren's eyes as his gaze raked him from head to toe did funny things to Taryn's stomach. There were nerves there still and something more. He couldn't name it exactly, but he was glad that the snug trousers kept his cock in check.

"We seem to match," he said, trying to break the spell of the unsettling attention.

The prince smiled and glanced at Kexen. "I don't suppose that's an accident."

The boy stared at his toes. "I do know your color preferences, your highness."

Finding out that his ensemble was intended to complement his husband's as well as suit his own style didn't bother Taryn. His fate was now tied to this powerful man, and anything that confirmed to everyone else that he belonged to Soren could only serve to protect him. He knew the Moorcondians prowling the corridors of the palace weren't going to take kindly to him, not after all the grief his father had caused the bordering towns.

He swished his skirt to show off the way his trousers peeked out. "Is this acceptable, do you think?"

Soren nodded. "As I said, beautiful—the perfect marriage of your station to your sex, I would say." The prince's praised warmed him, even as he wished he didn't care what this man thought. "There is only one thing missing." Soren lifted one hand and a pendant hung from his fingers. "Turn around, if you please."

Taryn did as he'd been told, his heart pounding for no discernable reason. The touch of Soren's fingers as he draped the necklace around Taryn's throat sent a strange sizzling sensation across his entire body. He missed the contact the moment Soren stepped back, although the man didn't go far. He loomed over Taryn from behind as they both looked into the mirror.

"This is from my family's collection. Nora finds it too plain to wear, but I think it just right for you."

Taryn stroked the pendant with the tip of one finger. The jewel itself was an oval, light blue gem in a bevel setting, hanging from a thin sliver chain that placed it in the middle of his breastbone. "It's lovely."

"It's a sapphire and platinum."

Kexen made a small squeal. When they both looked at him, he blushed a deep red and bowed low. "Forgive me. It's a very rare metal. I thought it might be silver, which would be very precious indeed, but others in the court will recognize it as platinum and be ever so jealous and… I'll shut up now." He bowed again.

The moment brought levity to Taryn's mood, even though it was at his poor groomer's expense. "I shall be very careful with it. Thank you," he added, glancing at Soren, yet unable to hold his gaze.

The man surprised him by taking one hand and planting a slow, soft kiss on the inside of his wrist. "I am proud to introduce you to court, my dear. Let us go."

With that, Soren led him into the hallway and through the palace. He held their hands aloft in a formal way, showing all they passed that they were a couple. There was much bowing and curtsying, but almost everyone was a servant or soldier. The powerful people of the palace were nowhere to be seen because they had all congregated for the banquet. The moment the massive doors were opened by the liveried guards on either side, it seemed as if a million pairs of eyes trained on them. Taryn knew a moment of panic. Soren's grip tightened enough to make Taryn feel grounded, safe. He wasn't going to have to face this intimidating crowd on his own. In this, he could rely on Soren.

They paused at the threshold as the chattering of those staring at them died out. Some officious-looking man announced their arrival in a way that made Taryn wince inwardly.

"Their most royal highnesses, Prince and Princess Soren of Moorcondia, Duke and Duchess of Vostguard."

Taryn supposed he really needed to get used to being referred to as a woman. They weren't going to change generations of tradition simply to placate his sensibilities. Besides, there was nothing demeaning meant by it. He was Soren's wife, so it followed that he would be given the courtesy titles that went with that position. If the worst thing in the rest of his life was to be called a princess, he could deal with it and keep his mouth shut. The more he had time to consider his fate, the more he realized how critical this treaty was for his people. This was his sacrifice — and no real hardship at all.

They proceeded down the path made by the court attendees, each showing the proper respect as they passed. Now that he was inside the room, he could see it was an antechamber, not the dining hall. People had gathered here in advance of eating. He wondered if that was the norm or something special for this occasion. That thought fled in the face of the two people waiting for them at the end of the gauntlet. They were a relatively young couple, dressed more elaborately than anyone else in the room, which was saying something. Taryn was doubly glad to have had Kexen to dress him. His clothing was a more refined version of the others' garments, yet still something he was proud to wear.

Soren stopped them a few feet away and bowed low. "Your majesties, may I present my bride, Taryn of the Marshlands."

Those royal eyes trained on him, and a feeling of panic rose within him once more. He hadn't thought about the proper way for him to greet the king and queen. Neither bowing nor curtsying seemed right. In the split second he had to figure it out, he did a little of both, with head down and one knee bent. His cheeks heated with embarrassment at his awkwardness, but at least he hadn't landed face-first on the stone floor.

There was a moment of utter silence before the king stepped toward them. "Welcome to the family, little brother." And with that simple sentence, the king brushed aside at least one of Taryn's worries. That was a signal to all that Taryn, notwithstanding his titles, was male and to be addressed as such. The king opened his arms. "Shall we go in for dinner? I, for one, am starving."

Chapter Five

Soren normally hated having to eat in the king's dining hall, preferring to take a private meal with friends or sitting around the cook's tent with his men. Banquets were their own special kind of torture. Not this night, though, because he loved watching Taryn eat. Most everything served was new to the boy, the Marshers being poor in resources as they were. His delight in each dish he tried was infectious. The only thing that marred the experience was that more often than not, Taryn turned to Nora, who sat on his other side, to ask questions about what everything was. Soren would have liked to perform that task himself, but he had to be understanding about it all. His daughter held no hint of threat nor dominion over Taryn, so it was easy for him to be open with her. Soren, as his husband, was a different matter altogether. That was especially true given that tonight was the first one of their being truly alone. If Soren let himself think about it too much, his dick was going to punch through his trousers.

"Oh what's this?" Taryn's eyes lit up at the sight of the entertainers entering the dining hall.

"Jugglers and dancers," Nora answered. "Wait until you see that blonde woman back there. She can contort her body into all manner of positions. It's quite impressive. Do you not have such entertainment in the Marshlands?"

Taryn shook his head. "Well, we do have a juggler, but he's not very good, and occasionally, wandering minstrels give us a show for a bit of food and wine. We don't have much of anything else, really. My father doesn't encourage any activity that doesn't serve a useful purpose, and not many outsiders are willing to venture into the Marshlands. The treaty will change that, hopefully." He glanced in Soren's direction.

The mere sight of those bright, green eyes was intoxicating. Something of his thoughts must have shown through as he stared back at his bride, because Taryn's cheeks pinked up and he swiftly looked away.

Nursing a goblet of wine, Soren leaned back in his chair and watched Taryn some more. The boy was much more entertaining than the performers. The way he laughed and clapped at the smallest things proved that growing up as Hogard's son hadn't destroyed his sweet nature. Soren was glad to be able to give his new wife the pleasures he deserved, inside and outside of bed.

But as the celebration wound down and the king and queen rose to signal its end, Taryn's expression turned wary. Soren, however, eagerly stood, extending his hand to guide Taryn up. The boy glanced at Soren with barely banked nervousness as he took the proffered hand. Soren kissed the inside of his wife's wrist as he'd done at the beginning of the evening, trying to reassure him without saying anything in front of eager listeners.

Taryn didn't offer up any reason for gossip, either, bidding the royal couple good night with his adorable mix of bowing and curtsying. As they left the dining hall, then the reception room, his wife did him proud by keeping his head held high and a pleasant expression on his face. That didn't change until they entered his sitting room. The boy managed to slip his hand from Soren's clasp without making it look as if he loathed the touch. A grinning Kexen greeted them in the bedroom.

"Good evening, your highness, your grace. I trust the evening went well?"

Taryn smiled. "It was wonderful, actually."

Soren was glad to hear it, although it could have been merely for the servant's benefit. Still, he chose to take is as truth and added in his own judgment. "Indeed, it was." He focused on his wife. "I shall give you time to prepare for bed and join you shortly."

Taryn's face betrayed little of his thoughts, but Soren detected a slight stiffening. The boy nodded before giving his attention to his groomer, effectively turning his back on his husband. Sensing his bride might benefit from time alone with someone who could calm his nerves, Soren continued to his own bedroom without further hesitation. Deward, his valet since Soren had become old enough to leave his nurse behind, rose from where he'd been sitting by the fire and put down the book he'd been reading. This was familiar territory. Both he and the valet were creatures of habit and transitioned into the usual ritual of Soren being undressed.

"I understand congratulations are in order, your highness?"

"Oh?"

"The duchess' introduction to the court was a triumph — or so I've heard."

Soren waited with impatience as the man went about securing the belt and sword in their usual place on the wall. When the valet returned to remove the tunic, he pressed him for more information. "Is that what is being said below stairs?"

The palace servants were a world almost unto themselves. Gossip traveled like wildfire, and they could make a highborn person's life at court a delight or a misery if they so chose — in subtle ways to avoid castigation for it. Although strictly speaking, it didn't matter to Taryn's station what the servants thought of him, Soren wanted his wife to have as many allies as possible within the palace.

"Yes, your highness. He was all that anyone talked about in the servant's dining hall. The pages relayed updates throughout the evening. Of course, your personal guards and campaigning cooks had already voiced their admiration. So, there was no expectation otherwise, even under the unusual circumstances of your union."

Deward dealt with the tunic and followed Soren as he sat for his boots to be removed. Decorum dictated that he be affronted that his wife was a subject of gossip, but knowing how hard this all was for Taryn, he wanted to hear more to ease his own concerns. "What about him found favor?"

Deward grunted as Soren pushed against the man's backside to aid in getting the damn ceremonial boots off. "Well, your highness, in addition to admiration for how well the duchess adapted to young Kexen's sartorial *imagination*, the words 'kind', 'respectful' and 'appreciative' were bandied about." After removing the other boot, he faced Soren. "There was no hint of disrespect or amusement at the duchess' situation or his origin. Everyone understands how difficult it must be for a Marsher boy to adjust to a new life in the palace as a member of the royal family — and as a wife, at that. He will be looked after," the man added before reaching for the buttons of Soren's trousers.

"Thank you for telling me, Deward." He wanted to say more, such as it was a relief to know that he didn't have to keep an eye on his wife for fear of trouble. But that kind of honest vulnerability wasn't permissible for a member of the royal family. So, he kept his mouth shut tight and slipped his arms into the dressing gown Deward held out for him.

Something in the right pocket hit his hip bone. "What is this?" he asked, touching the outside.

Deward kept his gaze downward. "A small vial of oil, your highness."

"Ah." Really, he shouldn't be surprised. His valet thought of everything. "Thank you. I'm sure the ever-thoughtful Kexen will have taken care of that, as well, but I'm happy to have it, nevertheless."

Soren walked slowly back to the duchess' bedroom, hoping that Taryn was ready for him. Well, as ready as the boy could be given his current dislike of the marriage bed. *I will change that tonight.*

Taryn was tucked in already, his arms over the covers. A vial of oil larger than the one in Soren's pocket sat conspicuously on the nightstand next to him. Kexen stood by the door, and the moment he saw Soren, he slipped out into the hall. Soren knew that

Deward would also be gone from the suite of rooms. He was alone with his bride, who lay there, staring up at the ceiling.

Soren approached the bed, undoing the sash of his robe as he went. "I don't want you to be afraid of me."

Taryn didn't look at him as he said, "I'm not. I know what you intend to do, and while I don't like it, I'm hoping it will be less painful than before. I'll get used to it, regardless. I understand my duty," he added, with only a hint of bitterness.

Soren dropped his robe onto the floor and slipped under the covers quickly so that his hard cock wouldn't get between him and the conversation he needed to have with his bride. He propped himself on one elbow to look at Taryn.

"What happens in this bed should be more than duty, and there shouldn't be any pain. I'm sorry I was so brutal that first night. With the treaty at stake, I hope you understand I couldn't indulge either of us by waiting until we got to know each other better. And I was inconsiderate the next morning. I misread certain signals." He sighed. "It had been a long journey to the Marshlands and the whole affair had been tense and uncertain, even with the treaty already hammered out. Plus, I wasn't expecting a male bride. The surprise threw me a little. None of that is an excuse," he hurried to add, "just an explanation."

Taryn still stared at the ceiling. "You don't have to apologize to me or justify your actions. I vowed fealty to you. That's effectively promising to obey."

Soren reached over slowly to run his fingers through strands of Taryn's hair. "I don't want a biddable wife. I would like someone more akin to a helpmate, someone with whom I can discuss the day and ask for advice, as well as give it."

Taryn did look at him now. "Was that how it was with your first wife?"

Soren allowed his sorrow to show a little bit. "Yes. We were well-matched as a couple. And even though our marriage was political, we fell in love with each other as children. We were lucky in that regard — as were my parents and the current king and queen."

"You don't love me." There was no recrimination in the statement, just bare fact, and Taryn went back to studying the ceiling, which had a beautiful mural, to be sure. Soren wished he were more interesting to his wife than the picture.

"We don't know each other well enough for that. Maybe we will never fall in love, but we can enjoy each other's company and work toward the common goal of making the treaty work."

"I agree...about the treaty." The boy's eyes went wide. "I can see now how large your army is. If you wanted, you could decimate my people. I'm surprised you've shown such restraint so far."

Soren didn't bother to correct Taryn's perceptions. He hadn't seen more than a fraction of the full force. But that information wouldn't help his cause this night, only increase Taryn's anxiety. "No one here wants more bloodshed. The treaty will give your people what they need without it."

"Very true. Moorcondia has such bounty. There was more food at the banquet than I've seen in a year back home...and variety. I've never seen the like. The Marshlands make for poor farming, and many animals don't thrive in the dark, wet environment. Moorcondia can give my people so much."

Taryn turned his head again to study Soren. There was a look of resolve on his face. "I won't fight you. You can do as you please with me. It's the least I can do to help my people."

Soren grimaced before sliding closer. He cupped Taryn's smooth cheek. He'd been fortunate that his bride didn't seem to grow the kind of bushy beard the Marsher men were known for. That was a fleeting thought and not important compared to the noticeable flinch at his touch and the resolve to be brave in his wife's eyes. "What we do in this bed is not about the treaty. We've satisfied the legal requirements. Now is a time for us to explore each other and find common pleasure. A sexless marriage is not what I want. Do you?" It was a risky question, because he truly didn't know the answer.

"I suppose not." Taryn looked away. "I doubt I'll ever enjoy this, however."

Soren chuckled. "I like a challenge, and I'm quite confident I can prove you wrong…if you'll let me."

Taryn's fingers tightened their hold on the covers. "I've already said you can do as you like."

Not exactly the enthusiastic response he'd been hoping for, but it was his job to show his wife what fun could be had in bed. He and Merida had been equally inexperienced on their wedding night. At this point, though, he was the knowledgeable and hopefully skilled partner. "All right."

They had the whole night, and even more than that if they chose, so he schooled himself again to be patient. Because they would get nowhere with so many layers of cloth over Taryn, Soren removed the first of them by gently tugging the covers from the boy's fingers. He gave way with only a moment's resistance. Soon it was simply his body clad in a more masculine version of a shift than Soren had seen him in before. There was only a tantalizing bit of lower leg showing. Soren would have removed that last impediment to please himself, but it would be too much too soon for his bride.

He started with the most basic thing for a man to do for his wife. Framing Taryn's face with his hands, he leaned over and kissed him. His bride's lips were soft and inviting, whether Taryn intended them to be or not. It was no hardship to taste only that part of the boy and find immense pleasure in it. Soren angled his body to align their mouths better. When he sensed a softening in Taryn, he begged entrance into that sweet mouth with his tongue. The resistance was token, and soon Soren was exploring that welcoming warmth with ease. Whether Taryn realized it or not, his body was already responding in a way that boded well.

Soren kept up this gentle assault, moving from mouth to just lips, then peppering the corners and jaw line with quick pecks and the occasional lick. In Soren's loose hold, his bride shuddered, and a low moan arose out of him. Soren couldn't keep the smile off his face as he increased his ardor. He plundered Taryn's mouth now, delighted when the boy's tongue met his for a playful chase. He moved to straddle the boy, then rucked up the shift. Although it would have been better to get the damn thing entirely off, Soren didn't dare break the kiss and the spell of their lovemaking by doing so. He settled for exposing the boy's chest, giving his lips access to new flesh.

With so little contact during their journey, he'd barely glimpsed Taryn's smooth and hairless torso. Once again, he gave fleeting thanks that his bride wasn't the typical Marsher lad. Then he moved his kisses down his bride's throat and over to his pecs. No breasts, naturally, which was a shame, as Soren had a great love of that womanly attribute. But Taryn's nipples were clearly no less sensitive when Soren latched his lips on first one, then the other, and sucked. Taryn's moans grew louder, and he arched into Soren's mouth. Even better, his cock bumped into something equally hard. His attention to his bride was having the desired effect. A nice feature of bedding a man was that arousal was easy to detect.

Soren picked up the pace, trailing his tongue down the middle of Taryn's chest and stomach until he reached the head of Taryn's shaft. It was small and slender, like everything else about his bride's body. A pearl of cum welled up from the slit. Holding Taryn down by grasping his narrow hips, Soren sucked that dick down into his mouth. As expected, his bride nearly levitated off the bed, and the cry the boy made was just what Soren had been hoping to elicit. He grinned around the hard length, using his tongue to tease the bundle of nerves underneath the cockhead.

Taryn brought his hand down on Soren's head and pushed feebly. "Stop. This isn't necessary." His voice was charmingly breathless.

Soren ignored the silly remark that he knew was remnants of the nonsense fed to the boy his whole life. It wasn't exactly a demand that he stop, and his bride's body was giving Soren the permission to proceed. Besides, Taryn had said he wouldn't fight him. Let the boy think this was purely for Soren's amusement. And there was no denying that Soren did love sucking his bride's dick. It had been very disappointing when Taryn had refused him during the journey home. Soren had been thinking of this moment for days now. He wasn't about to give up the experience.

He used one hand to grip the base of Taryn's cock, sensing that the boy might come too soon. There was more fun to be had for the both of them, but if Taryn found his release early, it would make the rest more difficult. It was awkward, but Soren managed to reach for the vial of oil without letting go of the dick with either hand or mouth. He popped the stopper with his thumb and tipped oil onto his fingers, not caring that it dripped. Sex was messy, and someone else would deal with it later. That was one of the benefits of being a prince. With his fingers now slick, he reached under Taryn and pressed against his hole.

Taryn instantly tensed beneath him, digging his fingers into Soren's scalp. But Soren had known this would happen, so he didn't do more than circle the puckered ring while continuing to use his tongue to stoke Taryn's arousal. Soon his bride relaxed again, enough that Soren dared to slip one finger into Taryn's tight channel. He didn't waste any time showing his bride how much pleasure this part of his body could give him. He swept the pad of his fingertip over that special place that made men wild. Taryn didn't disappoint, bucking under him, his breath coming out in staccato bursts.

When Soren sensed a softening of Taryn's hole, he slipped a second finger in and started fucking his bride with them while continuing to suck and lave the boy's cock. And as delightful as it was to experience his wife's new-found sexuality, soon he couldn't wait any longer. His cock strained to join in the fun, and his balls ached with the need for release. He let go of his grip on Taryn's cock and swallowed him down. The boy cried out and arched his back as he came. Soren worked the shaft with this throat muscles to wring the last bit of cum before letting the dick go. At the same time, he pulled out his fingers and swiftly positioned Taryn with his legs bent. The boy's body still shuddered from his orgasm as Soren pushed his cock past the spasming ring and fed it as far as it would go. He grunted at the feel of the tight channel and knew he wouldn't last long himself.

Not wanting to give Taryn any time to tense up again, Soren leaned over and claimed his bride's mouth once more. He fucked him with his tongue and his dick in short, hard thrusts. He groaned long and loud as his own climax overtook him. Something warm splashed his abdomen and he knew in that moment that his bride had come again, simply from having his ass fucked. Soren pushed his cock farther into Taryn's channel and growled in satisfaction. He ground their pelvises together as he milked the last of his cum before collapsing on top of his bride.

* * * *

"You don't have to do that."

Soren took his eyes off his task of wiping the cum from Taryn's chest to look at him. "I want to. This will get itchy if you let it dry on your skin." Satisfied that he'd done a good job, Soren moved to do the same to Taryn's ass.

Taryn reached out to place a hand on Soren's arm. "You really don't have to do *that*."

Soren grinned at his wife's modesty. "Once again, I want to. And I bet you hate the feeling of my cum leaking from your hole."

Taryn blushed as he snatched his hand away. "I don't suppose I'll ever convince you not to do something."

"You might. I invite you to try." He kept his tone light and teasing. The night had turned out even better than he'd hoped. *I made my bride come – twice!* When he was finished, he tossed the soiled cloth on top of Taryn's shift on the floor, which had become dirty with cum as well.

Taryn made as if he were going to get up. "We shouldn't leave those there."

Soren eased him back down on the mattress. "Of course, we should. A maid will see to it tomorrow."

Taryn's expression turned mulish. "That hardly seems fair."

"Oh?" Soren climbed onto the bed and slid his bride over so that he could lie beside him. "Why not? It's their job. None of them try to take my place in battle because that's mine. We all have our place, Taryn." He pulled the covers over both of them and tugged Taryn into his embrace.

There was a token resistance before his bride laid his head on Soren's shoulder. "They'll know what we did."

Soren had to stifle a laugh. His bride really was adorable in his parochial views. "Yes, they will, and it's no different than what they'll encounter in nearly every chamber of the members of my brother's court. It's expected, and again, it will ease people's worries to know that we are enjoying our marriage bed."

"I understand." Taryn's tone implied that wasn't really true. "I guess I also understand why you insisted I suck your cock every day on the journey. It does feel good."

Soren stroked the boy's head. "It feels amazing. Aren't you sorry now that you refused my offers to reciprocate?"

"Maybe." There was silence for a few seconds before the boy spoke again. Apparently he was in a talkative mood, which suited Soren just fine. After-sex cuddling and conversation was a favorite time for him. "Are you going to come here every night?"

"Yes. I meant it when I said I was a man of strong appetites. I might even coax you up here during the day sometimes." Taryn gave a small gasp and tried to lift his head. Soren held it firmly on his shoulder. He was enjoying this interlude far too much.

Taryn gave up easily and eased back onto him. "Is that because I'm a boy, and you think I want sex all the time, too?"

Soren chuckled. "No. It's because you're my wife and married people often want as much of each other as they can get in the beginning. Merida and I could hardly keep our hands off each other," he added, even though the thought of her left a twinge of pain in his heart. They had always lain like this and talked after sex.

"Oh. Well, I said I'd give you whatever you want, and it was…very pleasurable." The boy was silent for a while longer, then, "Can I ask you a question?"

"Always."

Taryn reached up and stroked Soren's left hand with his own. "I noticed other men at the banquet, as well as their wives, had a ring like I do. Why aren't you wearing one?"

Soren thought of the ring that Merida had given him and how long it had taken him to be ready to remove it after her death. "Wedding bands are exchanged during the ceremony, usually."

Taryn stilled. "I was supposed to give you a ring?"

Hearing the dismay in his wife's tone, Soren hugged him close and hurried to ease his mind. "No. That's not a Marsher custom, is it? And you weren't supposed to be my bride anyway. You couldn't have known that."

"I feel bad about it, though. I don't have any money to buy you one now."

Soren squeezed his bride for a moment and kissed him on the top of his head for good measure. "My dear, you have a great deal of money. As my duchess, a sum was settled on you the moment we married. Nora will gladly go over it with you."

"But that's *your* money!"

"No. It's the duchy's money, and by law, it's yours to do with as you please. Now, as lovely as this is, it's late and the day was long. Go to sleep. We'll talk more in the morning, if you wish."

There was no reply, but Taryn's body went boneless and soon, his rhythmic breathing told Soren that his bride had fallen asleep. Feeling more hopeful that he had in many days, Soren did the same.

* * * *

Taryn woke facing his husband, their two erect cocks held in the man's grip as he stroked them hard and fast. Taryn was coming even before his brain truly registered what was going on, and as with the previous night, the orgasm hit him like a raging storm, buffeting him about and leaving him limp. "Gods," he said when he had his breath back. "Do you intend to wake me every morning like that?"

Soren answered him first with a passionate kiss that robbed Taryn of his breath. "That and other ways," Soren said before sliding out of bed. He was donning his sleeping robe when there was a tentative knock on the door. "That will be Kexen to help you with your morning ablutions. Come to my suite when you are ready. We're breaking our fast there."

Still reeling from his abrupt and pleasurable awakening, Taryn sat up and called out. "Come in."

Kexen entered with arms full of clothing and a big grin on his face. "Good morning, your grace. How was your night?"

Taryn blew hair out of his eyes. "I think you know the answer to that already." His nose twitched at the strong smell of his and Soren's spending.

Kexen chuckled. "Yes, I do, your grace." He brought a robe over and held it out. "Here… Let's get you cleaned up a bit before you join the prince."

Taryn slipped his arms through the sleeves. "I find this all very embarrassing." Even though he'd known this Moorcondian boy for less than a day, he felt he could confide in him. He needed a friend in this vast, strange place.

The boy led him to the garderobe. "Nonsense, your grace. It's to be expected, and I'm happy for you." He stopped to peer at Taryn closely. "Should I be happy for you?"

Taryn smiled, then rolled his eyes. "Yes."

Kexen all but clapped with glee. "Wonderful!"

His personal groomer helped Taryn be presentable for breakfast before accompanying him to Soren's suite. The prince was already fully dressed and sitting at one end of a small table by the tall windows that covered the outside wall. He smiled when he saw Taryn and rose as he came over to sit. "Good morning, my dear. I hope you are hungry." He sat again once Kexen had seated Taryn at the other end. "I had Deward order up a variety of food for you to try."

Taryn looked at the spread before him. "I couldn't possibly eat this much." He looked at his husband with wide eyes. *Is the man trying to fatten me up?*

"Try what appeals to you and eat as much as you like. I promise you it won't go to waste. The kitchen staff will devour our leftovers."

Kexen hovered nearby with a pot of something that smelled delicious. "Would you like some hot chocolate, your grace?"

"I don't know what that is." Taryn was embarrassed at his own ignorance, but at least this setting felt like a safe place to show it.

Soren gestured for Kexen to pour. "You'll love it, I'll wager."

Taryn took a tentative sip and had to stifle a moan. "Oh, it's wonderful." His reaction obviously pleased Soren, and Taryn was surprised to find that he wanted to make Soren happy this morning.

"Excellent. Kexen, put hot chocolate in the 'yes' column of the breakfast ledger."

Taryn peered at his husband's cup. "Is that what you're drinking?"

"No. This is coffee. You are welcome to try it, but I don't think you will like it very much."

"I'll stick with this, then." No matter how wary he'd been of his husband, the man did seem to know what was best and act upon it. If nothing else, Taryn trusted his judgment. He sipped some more and perused the spread before him. All he had to do was gesture toward a platter or bowl, and Kexen immediately served some up on Taryn's plate. It was all very tasty. If he was supposed to pick among them for his breakfast going forward, he would be hard pressed.

Soren was sifting through some papers as he ate. "You can have whatever you want each day, my dear." He looked at him from across the table. "Just tell Kexen in advance. We Moorcondians expect variety in our meals," he added before returning to his papers. "So many meetings today," he said with a shake of his head. "That's what happens when one is away for many days, I suppose."

Kexen approached Taryn once more, carrying a silver tray with a mound of brightly colored envelopes. "Your mail, your grace."

Taryn blinked at him while he swallowed his mouthful of food. "My *what*?"

Soren answered. "They're invitations, my dear. Everyone at court wants to meet the new Duchess of Vostguard personally and curry his favor. You need not accept them all. I'm sure Kexen can help you navigate the politics behind each of them. That being said, you really should open the large red one first."

Taryn plucked the envelope off the tray and accepted the small, sharp blade that Kexen drew from a scabbard on his belt. "Who is it from? Do you know?" He broke the heavy wax seal.

"My grandmother. She is very fond of that color, and no one dares use it for their own envelopes for fear it will be taken as impudence."

"Oh." Taryn nearly fumbled the card that he tugged free. The lettering was ornate and done in black ink. He frowned, having a little bit of trouble reading the elaborate script. "She's inviting me to tea?" He looked at Soren. "What's that?" Once again, he felt like the ignorant Marsher boy that he was.

If Soren was annoyed at his question, he didn't show it. "It's a drink like coffee or chocolate. Not to my tastes, but many people like it. And in this case, it is served in the late afternoon with dainty sandwiches and delicate pastries."

Taryn wasn't sure he truly understood the custom, but the idea of meeting the dowager queen gave him a nervous stomach. "Do you have tea with her?"

Soren raised his eyebrows. "When summoned, yes. The last time was right before I left for the Marshlands. My grandmother reminded me to be kind and patient with my new bride. I fear I did not take her sage advice to heart, as I should have," he added with a fleeting frown.

Sensitive to their audience, Taryn felt compelled to disagree. "Of course, you did."

Soren nodded. "Thank you, my dear. In any event, you needn't worry about the command performance. This is her way of getting to know you. She doesn't bite," he added with a quick grin. "Although she does have a cutting tongue," he said, almost under his breath.

Taryn heard the echo of the squire's words saying the very same thing. It didn't help his bout of nerves any. He tossed the missive back on the tray and sat back with his cup of chocolate in hand. "I don't know what to wear."

"I'm sure Kexen will sort that all out."

The boy nodded eagerly. "The head seamstress is ready whenever it pleases you, your grace."

Soren stood. "See? Nothing to fret about." He surprised Taryn by coming over and lifting his chin up with one hand. "I shall see you later." Then he kissed him briefly on the lips and strode out of the room.

Taryn was left with Kexen and the dour-looking Deward, who quietly cleared the prince's dishes. Because the drink filled him more than he'd expected, Taryn ate very little of the food before declaring himself done. He felt guilty about how much was left. It could have fed a large Marsher family for the day. But Soren had said it wouldn't go to waste, so he resolved not to worry about it. There were more pressing matters to occupy his thoughts.

"I suppose we should get going," he said, pushing his chair back and standing.

"Other than the dowager queen, people wait on your pleasure, your grace."

While Taryn appreciated Kexen's friendly reminder, he still didn't want to be rude, no matter how low on the social ladder someone else was. He headed back to his own suite and to the bathing chamber. "Well, that may be, but I must get clean before I'll feel fit for company. Let's not dawdle, Kexen."

"Yes, your grace." The boy hurried to make the preparations.

For the first time that morning, Taryn was alone. He took the moment to consider how he felt after his night of passion with his husband. There was a sweet ache in his ass, but nothing like the sting of the previous time. The mere thought of what he'd done in bed with another man caused his cock to twitch.

"None of that now," he admonished himself in a low voice. "I have to see the seamstress, whatever that's going to entail, and I can't be hard when I bathe, either." Confident he had himself under control, he continued on his way, trying not to imagine what the next night would bring.

Chapter Six

Taryn tried not to gawk as he followed Kexen through the palace. His personal groomer had somehow managed to lead from behind and had looked aghast at Taryn's suggestion that the boy simply go ahead of him. Apparently one of the rules of his new station was that no one beneath him in rank should precede him. He wasn't sure he was ever going to get used to the idea that he had somehow become an important person. As he walked down the exquisite halls, he couldn't help but feel out of place. That was true even though his new clothing made him look more regal than he would have expected for everyday wear. The green kirtle mirrored the style from the night before, but with sleeves this time, and the trousers were of the same soft material. Kexen had called it cotton, and it was almost as lovely as silk and velvet. The fabric moved with him — freeing, not binding or stiff, nor was it itchy. He enjoyed the feel of it against his skin.

He still couldn't understand why it was so critical to go order more clothing this morning. Apparently, he needed a new outfit for his tea with the dowager queen. When he'd suggested that he could simply wear what he already had on, Kexen's expression had been so appalled that it was as if Taryn had proffered that he could go naked. The boy had explained with the kind of slow, clear speech that one might use with a very small and not particularly clever child that Moorcondian people of power changed their clothing throughout the day to match whatever they were doing. It seemed a waste of time and material. What would these people who snuck peeks of him as he passed think of how he'd often worn the same clothes for days on end? At least he and Kexen were headed for the ground floor, a place where the servants went about their daily business. Taryn would feel more comfortable around such simple folk. And he had insisted on this journey instead of making the seamstress and her helpers haul many bolts of cloth up to his chambers. He hoped he never reached a point in which he was indifferent to making ridiculous work for others.

"How many floors are there?" Taryn wanted to learn the layout of the palace as quickly as possible. Dragging Kexen around with him everywhere wasn't going to be practical. He needed to be more independent throughout the day. *That's assuming Kexen isn't my jailer.* It was important to remember that he was as much a hostage to the treaty as a pampered consort of a prince.

Kexen pulled almost even with him. "Four, your grace. This is the first floor, where all the public rooms are for the palace residents and their visitors to meet and socialize, as well as the throne room and the great dining hall."

"Yes, I was there last night for the banquet, but I must confess I wasn't paying attention to where my husband took me."

"Navigating the palace takes some getting used to. It will become easier quickly. You really don't need to learn the layout of more than this floor and the second one, where the chambers are for the royal family and higher-ranking officials. The top floor is for servants and lower-ranking residents. You won't have a need to go there. And after this one trip, the basement floor is also not somewhere you will ever visit."

Taryn turned his head to glance in Kexen's direction. "You don't know that. Perhaps I'll want to go to the kitchen for a bite to eat."

Kexen actually gasped. "Your grace, you'll do no such thing! If you want something to eat, I or another servant will bring it to you."

Taryn shook his head. "That seems like an awful inconvenience just because I want a slice of bread with cheese, or something."

Kexen sniffed. "You are the Duchess of Vostguard. I will gladly bring you bread and cheese or anything else you desire every hour on the hour if that is what you want."

That show of devotion made Taryn very uncomfortable, but before he could think of a suitable, if futile, reply, a group of five women approached him from one of the many intersections of the hall. Each one was dressed far more elaborately than he was and flashed large, painted fans in front of their faces as they walked. The fans were nothing like the ones Marsher women made out of large leaves to shoo insects away from food. These were purely decorative and being waved in a performative way that he supposed was meant to be coy. Gods, he hoped that wasn't part of the female style he was supposed to adopt. He didn't relish the idea of putting his attention into such frippery, given that he could barely walk without tripping on his long skirts as it was.

The obvious leader of the group, an exquisite woman with honey-blonde hair, came within a few feet of him before executing a flawless and deep curtsy. The woman's bodice barely contained her bounty as she did so. Taryn feared he would be given a full view of them if she didn't rise quickly, which she did with a snap of her fan. The others followed suit, although failing to match the flair.

"Your grace, welcome to the palace. I saw you from afar at the banquet last night, yet couldn't manage to approach you."

Taryn effected his curtsy bow, feeling far more awkward than he had before. "You have me at a disadvantage, madam." There... That sounded almost confident. There was something about the way the woman looked at him that made him very uncomfortable. Her eyes didn't quite mirror her friendly expression.

"I am Lady Balter. Fiona to my friends." She leaned in, sending a waft of cloying perfume Taryn's way. "And I do hope we will become friends, your grace. The palace can be a lonely place." She spread her lips in a smile that once again didn't reach her eyes.

Taryn knew there was no chance that he would ever find the company of these women to his liking. Whatever it was they did all day, he couldn't imagine engaging in it. Still, he knew how to respond. His people weren't entirely without social graces. "You are too kind, Lady Balter."

"*Fiona*, please." She gestured with her fan toward the women behind her. "We're heading to a card room. Why not join us so we can get to know each other?"

Not certain of what exactly one did in such a place, Taryn tried to find the best way to beg off. He didn't get the chance. Kexen inserted himself into the conversation without actually getting any closer to them. "Your pardon, Lady Balter, but the duchess has an engagement this morning that can't wait. I'm sure you understand. Your grace?" The boy got Taryn moving around the group of women, once more without actually touching him. Lady Balter's gasp of outrage carried down the hallway.

Kexen waited until he and Taryn were walking down a set of wide stairs before saying anything more. "I'm sorry, your grace, but even if the seamstresses were not waiting for our visit, I would have made an excuse to get you away from that...*lady*. She is not someone you want to befriend."

"Why not? She seemed..." He couldn't think of a way of describing Balter in favorable terms.

"She is a viper and would love to make you look bad. Nothing she ever says to you will be sincere."

"I don't understand."

Kexen stopped abruptly at the bottom of the stairs and urged Taryn into a recess in the wall. "She was Prince Soren's lover before he left to marry you." The boy kept his voice low.

Taryn's heart sank at the news. He'd known that Soren had an active sex life. The man had said as much more than once. Coming face-to-face with one of those lovers reminded him of how inadequate he was compared to what a woman could offer. No matter what he wore, he was never going to present the same enticing image as Lady Balter's décolletage.

"She's his lover?" He hated how insecure he sounded. Thank the gods it was only Kexen. If that boy had a dishonest or disloyal bone in his body, it was impossible to detect.

"*Was*, your grace. Past tense. Everyone knows the prince is a faithful husband. It's killing her that he came back with someone she thinks pales in comparison to her." Kexen leaned in closer. "Word is that she tried to use your...*lack* of femininity to woo him back and was soundly rejected."

Hearing this made Taryn feel a bit better. Of course, Soren might merely be being true to his code of conduct and not because he thought Taryn was as desirable in bed as that woman. He didn't voice his insecurity, however. Kexen was doing his best to alleviate his worries. He made light of the situation instead.

"Is there anything that happens in this palace that you don't know about?"

Kexen gave him a cheeky grin. "I don't think so, your grace. Shall we?" He motioned for Taryn to walk down the hallway to his left.

This part of the palace was decorated more simply but was still magnificent compared to his father's longhouse. And people were obviously working, walking briskly by with purpose, taking only a second to acknowledge him with a quick bob of their head or shallow curtsy. Taryn felt far more at ease here, although the bustling noise of the seamstress' room almost overwhelmed him. It was filled with mostly women sitting at long tables, cloth everywhere and fingers flying as people worked to create what he assumed where outfits for the royal family and other important palace inhabitants. He really hated adding to their workload, but apparently even when it came to what he put on his body, he had no say in the matter.

A middle-aged woman, well-groomed, yet simple in attire, hurried over to them. She bobbed a perfunctory curtsy before speaking. "Welcome, your grace. We are honored by your presence."

"Thank you, madam, but please don't let me disrupt your business." He rather feared that the others were about to rise to greet him, and that wouldn't do at all. With the amount of bowing and curtsying that went on in the palace, it was surprising that anyone got anything done. *Such a waste of time*, but he understood he had little power to stop someone from doing it. It wasn't his place to change their ways. It was his duty to conform to theirs.

The woman smiled. "Thank you, your grace. With the coming balls, we have many orders to fill."

Taryn tried to hide his horror. "Balls?" Gods help him. Was he supposed to *dance* with Soren?

Perhaps sensing his alarm, Kexen intervened once more. "Mistress Camilla, may we see what material you have set aside for the duchess' approval?"

"Of course, this way." As with Kexen, the woman had a way of guiding Taryn where she wanted him to go without actually taking the lead.

They arrived at a table in the far corner against a row of windows that gave view to an inner courtyard of some sort. Taryn's gaze was immediately drawn to that, but he knew he was supposed to be looking at the stuff on the table. Maybe if he was attentive enough, he could finish this chore quickly and take a walk outside. *Am I even allowed to leave the building?* He wasn't exactly a prisoner, but he also knew that his life wasn't his to command anymore—not that it ever had been.

The seamstress held up two pieces of partially sewn red clothing. "I thought these might make the perfect ensemble for the duchess' tea with Queen Margrette this afternoon."

"How did she know about that?" Taryn couldn't help asking his groomer in a low voice.

"I sent a page ahead with the news while you bathed, your grace." Kexen's reply was at a normal level, showing no unease at including Mistress Camilla in the exchange.

"Just so," the woman joined in. "With such urgency, I needed to find something suitable that could be finished in only a few hours." She held a long-sleeved kirtle aloft that was red velvet. "See how this has a high, rounded collar? It was ordered for a young lord about to make his debut at court, so the measurements fit your grace's...*slender* frame quite well."

In other words, Taryn was physically akin to a pubescent Moorcondian boy. He supposed he should find it embarrassing, and he might grow a bit more in the next few years, but he was never going to be tall or large. Maybe that was for the best and a design of the gods, given that he was now living the life of a royal woman.

"It is beautiful," was all he said, because he didn't want this woman to feel bad about anything. None of his predicament was her fault. "And it's in the dowager queen's favorite color."

The seamstress treated him to a broad smile. "My very thought, your grace." She laid the kirtle on the table once more and used two hands to show off the other garment. "These satin trousers were made for

Lord Fennel. See how it's a darker shade of red? It will go wonderfully with the kirtle."

Kexen pursed his lips as he gazed at it. "Yes. It's perfect, Mistress Camilla. Well done. How lucky for us that Lord Fennel is such a dandy."

The woman beamed even brighter. "All we need to do is take in the width to make them hug the legs better and hem the cuffs to fit the duchess' height. It will be done in plenty of time to dress the duchess for the tea."

Taryn couldn't help interjecting. "Excuse me, but won't those who commissioned these clothes be put out by your giving them to me?"

Mistress Camilla froze for a moment, and her gaze slid toward Kexen before she answered. "They will be honored to have been of service, your grace, and won't have to wait long for us to make substitutes."

Taryn sighed inwardly. He might not know or understand Moorcondians, but it seemed to him that all he was really doing was making a nuisance of himself to others at the palace. "If you say so, madam."

The seamstress gestured to someone. "We need only take your measurements for the alterations, then we can discuss what other clothing you need and the materials you'll want. I hope my selections will please you, your grace."

"I'm sure they will." An easy thing to say, given that he didn't really care and wouldn't trust his own judgment in these matters, anyway. Kexen would be the one making the decisions.

Fortunately, the person who came to take his measurements was a boy, who whipped through it with little fanfare. Once it was done, he took the kirtle and trousers from the seamstress and raced away with them. The immediate needs having been taken care of,

Mistress Camilla tried to engage Taryn in a discussion about fabric and style. The bolts of cloth, with their various colors, textures and embellishments, made his head swim. He was overwhelmed with the choices within seconds. Kexen, naturally, was by his side, engaging the seamstress with questions and comments. The two of them became so absorbed by their own discussions that neither seemed to notice when Taryn walked away.

He approached a row of windows along one wall and looked out. Despite the lowest floor of the palace being partially underground, someone had been smart about the configuration of at least this room. Lots of light shone in, making the sewers' tasks easier. Even so, he imagined that they couldn't work much past the late afternoon without artificial light. A quick glance around told him that there were few candles to be had and none hung from the ceiling as they did on the two upper floors where he'd been. The people tasked with keeping the palace running must start very early in the morning to get anything done in a timely manner. No doubt, despite their efforts, there would be those in the palace who found them wanting, having no appreciation of the hard work that went into catering to their needs and whims alike.

I must never become like that.

Even as he thought it, he wasn't sure he could ever control his own demands. The idea that right at this moment, someone was working furiously to have his outfit ready for the afternoon tea saddened him. But he had no say in it, so all he could do was stay out of everyone's way. He put his arms on the window ledge and stared outside. The inner courtyard was only partially visible. It was huge and probably ran the inner ring of the entire building. But it also gave him a better view of a part of the palace that he'd hadn't seen yet since arriving. He'd been so filled with worry when Soren had carried him up the stairs to the entry, he hadn't had a chance to truly see where he was now going to live.

Almost directly across from where he stood was a tall, imposing section of the palace that was decorated differently than the rest. It was more somber and soared up so high that he couldn't quite see the top of it, no matter how much he craned his neck. His mood brightened as he thought he knew what it must be. A girl walked by him, and his curiosity overrode his desire to be unobtrusive.

"Excuse me, is that the library?" He pointed to the structure.

The girl stopped immediately and bobbed a curtsy. "Yes, your grace."

"Thank you." He turned back to the window and stared some more. He couldn't imagine how many books must be kept there or how they were arranged. His own meager collection had always been stacked one on top of the other, but Kexen had stood them against each other on a shelf in Taryn's sitting room. The library probably had such shelves, as well. Maybe all the walls in the library were covered with them on each of the many floors it must have. Certainly, there were more than the four floors of the palace.

Taryn's day suddenly brightened as he formed a plan of how he might spend the rest of his free time before taking tea with the dowager queen. With a lighter heart, he returned to the table where Kexen and Mistress Camilla were having a conversation about something called 'piping'. For once, Taryn didn't hesitate to interrupt.

"Kexen?" The groomer instantly looked at him. "When we are done here, I want to visit the library. Would you please arrange that for me?"

"There is no need, your grace. The Master of Books has already been told to expect a visit from you at any time. We can go whenever you like."

There was something unsettling about his needs being met without his even having to ask. Still, it would be churlish of him to resent it. "Excellent." Then he couldn't help adding, "Was that something you did?"

"No, your grace. I wouldn't presume. The prince did it and informed me."

Putting aside the confusing issue of where his groomer drew the line of what he could and couldn't presume about Taryn and his needs, there was a strange warmth within him hearing that Soren had thought of him so kindly at all. "I see."

He made an effort to focus on the discussion of his clothing but was unable to concentrate on something he cared so little about. Instead, he pictured how wonderful his trip to the library might be. He also tried to push aside thoughts of Soren. It proved difficult. This unwanted husband of his continued to surprise him. Soren could treat Taryn as a nuisance and a convenient place to satisfy his sexual urges—yet he wasn't. He'd been listening to Taryn when he'd spoken of his desire to use the library and had remembered and cared enough to ease the way for a visit.

A sweet ache deep inside Taryn still lingered where Soren had wrung from him a pleasure Taryn hadn't dared dream of and remained conflicted about. Those thoughts had the predictable result. As he clasped his hands in front of himself to hide his reaction, it occurred to him that he really needed to talk to Kexen about commissioning some male small clothes. It was all well and fine for women to wear shifts. Their bodies didn't betray them in such obvious ways. He wouldn't have thought his would, either. Soren's touch and the memories of it were proving him wrong. The idea of asking Kexen for such things was embarrassing, but he reminded himself that he was the Duchess of Vostguard. He could have what he wanted and shouldn't worry about what others thought.

Maybe if he said it often enough, he would actually believe it.

* * * *

Soren grimaced as the arrow let loose by the captain of the archers split his in two. Then he clapped the woman on the shoulder and congratulated her. "Well done, Willa. I can see you prove me right in my elevation of you." It was important to appreciate that he depended on his soldiers to be their best to keep each other and the kingdom safe.

The woman, who as nearly as tall as he was, gave him a cheeky grin. "Perhaps you need more practice, your highness. And being newly married, I suppose you might have trouble finding the time."

He chuckled. His soldiers knew not to pander to him, and he could take the friendly ribbing. He would have been disappointed if she'd tried to excuse his loss due to something other than her superior skill. "You're right. We'll compete again as soon as I feel ready — which should be sometime around *never*."

Willa and all of those around them laughed, as he'd intended them to do. With another clap on her shoulder, he passed his equipment over to Sam and walked away. Rolf followed at his heels. Soren intended to take his midday meal at the barracks dining hall, but through a nearby gate into the palace proper, he spotted a familiar figure. He took a moment to marvel at how little time it had taken for him to learn to recognize his unusual duchess at a distance. He stopped and watched as Taryn, with Kexen behind, walked quickly to the library.

"Of course," Soren muttered, rather pleased that he also understood his wife's desires.

Rolf stopped with him. "Your highness?"

"My wife has a fondness for books. I'll wager he'll stay in the library all afternoon before he needs to go meet my grandmother. It's nearly time for the midday meal. It won't do for him to skip it, given the how little food is served at tea." A thought occurred to him.

Whipping his head around, he bellowed, "Sam!"

His squire came running toward him, his hands free of Soren's archery equipment. "Yes, your highness?"

"Go to the kitchen and have them prepare a picnic lunch for me and the duchess. I shall meet you at the barracks." The boy nodded before racing off again. Soren smiled to himself at the plan. And his cock showed its usual enthusiasm anytime he thought of his new wife. He sniffed, however, and knew he couldn't approach Taryn smelling of sweat. "I need a bath," he tossed at Rolf before continuing on his way, except this time, he headed for the barracks bathing chamber.

* * * *

Taryn stood inside the entryway of the library, literally speechless. It was as he'd pictured it — soaring up with books lined on shelves like soldiers along three walls — yet also far more magnificent than his imagination could have conjured. It contained a hollow center fenced in with dark wooden railings that allowed him to look to the very top of the building. As with the sewing room, one wall contained nothing but windows all the way up its open floors, permitting sunlight to stream through. This place was unlike the rest of the palace, as well, being more somber and understated in its riches. A soothing quiet enveloped it in contrast to the constant bustle of the palace hallways and rooms. Everyone he saw walked without haste, yet seemingly with a purpose. If he'd ever thought there would be a perfect place in the world, this would be it. He briefly wondered if Soren would permit him to spend his days entirely within this library.

Kexen broke through his thoughts. "Your grace, this is Dame Edina, the Master of the Books."

Taryn dropped his gaze to see an older woman dressed in modest black approach him. She performed the usual ritual of greeting to his lofty status before presenting him with a silent and sober gaze. If she was supposed to fawn all over and entertain him, she was signaling that she'd do no such thing.

Taryn admired her instantly. "Good morning, madam. Thank you for taking time out of your busy day to greet me."

A look of surprise crossed the woman's face before she returned to a more passive one. "I am always happy to help a lover of books, your grace."

Taryn glanced around. "I have never seen the like. It's amazing." He gazed at her once more and dared to ask his biggest question. "How many books do you house here?"

Once again, the woman's face betrayed her surprise. He supposed that not many in the palace cared about such things. "This library houses over a million items, including drawings, personal papers and letters of prior people of note, maps and even some objects of art that need particular safeguarding."

Taryn's mind reeled at the information. "You must labor long and hard to maintain it all."

The Master of the Books let a quick smile show. "I have a very dedicated staff. I wish I had more," she added, surprisingly, but not with any real rancor. "How may I help you, your grace?"

Taryn had already given this issue some thought. "Do you have a concise history of Moorcondia?"

"We do. There are thousands of books that speak to that issue, naturally. But there is one very good one that provides a complete history, if not a very detailed one. Please settle yourself somewhere comfortable, and I will bring it to you."

Taryn dearly wanted to follow the woman to gawk some more and ask questions. Some subtle sign from Kexen reminded him that the Duchess of Vostguard was always to be catered to. "Thank you," he said instead and waited for Kexen to tell him where to go.

His personal groomer didn't disappoint. With his usual skill at shepherding Taryn around, Kexen brought him to a small alcove near the windows that held overstuffed couches. When Taryn sat, he was almost swallowed up by the upholstery but there was no denying its luxurious comfort. Soon, he thought nothing about the furniture at all when the Master of the Books brought him a weighty tome bound in leather and reeking of age. She handed it to him as if bestowing a great and precious gift.

Taryn accepted it with the care it deserved. "Thank you."

The woman nodded. "It is my pleasure, your grace. Keep it as long as you like. It doesn't contain information of the most recent generations of our great country, but it is a good primer of how we came to be. If you need anything else, please let me know."

With that, Dame Edina left. Taryn settled against the back of the couch and opened the first page. He was almost afraid he would be unable to read it, expecting an elaborate script much like the dowager queen's invitation. To his relief, the handwriting was clear, written in block letters that were surprisingly uniform in size and shape. He had never seen the like.

He held the book up to Kexen. "Who writes like this?"

The boy furrowed his brow for a second before answering. "Oh, it's typeset, your grace." Taryn's confusion must have shown on his face. "It's done through printing, ink laid on carved letters and imprinted on the paper. Do you, um, not have that in the Marshlands?"

Taryn put the book on his lap and ran his fingers across the page. "No, we have nothing like that. Are all the books here written this way?"

"The more recent ones, yes. I'm sure Dame Edina could explain the process better than I, your grace."

Taryn shook his head. Every day in smalls ways he was learning just how advanced the Moorcondians were compared to his people. The gravity of his duty to make the marriage and the treaty work pressed upon him once more. Determined not to be get mired into worry, he settled into the couch and began to read. It didn't take more than a few dozen pages before he questioned whether he really wanted to learn as much about his new home as he'd thought. The chapter told the story of the first treaty wife long ago, much like him.

And it hadn't end well for her at all.

* * * *

Soren found his bride right where Dame Edina had indicated, curled on a sofa, reading some large book. The boy looked utterly engrossed and comfortable, unlike Soren, who had rarely visited the library. He'd much the preferred outdoor activities suited to soldiers rather than his tedious studies and had relied on his tutors to get the books themselves and chase him down. As content as Taryn appeared, Soren knew he'd made the right call to find his wife and force him to eat something. The sight of him made Soren hard, too, which wasn't part of the plan, yet welcome all the same. If he were very clever and patient, he might be able to fill his bride in other ways than food.

Kexen lounged against the window ledge, attentive while reading something of his own. He looked up at Soren's approach and scurried off without hesitation when Soren gestured. Knowing how to be quiet, Soren came within a foot of Taryn and gazed upon his pretty head until the boy noticed his presence.

"Oh." Taryn straightened and shut his book. "I'm sorry. I didn't hear you."

"I'd be a poor soldier if I didn't know stealth."

Taryn looked at him from under his lashes. "Does that mean you see me as the enemy? Or prey, perhaps?"

There was almost a coyness in his wife's tone. Soren took it as teasing and gave some back. "You are a prize worth bagging, my dear."

Taryn's cheeks pinked, and he lowered his gaze to the book. "Was I supposed to meet you now?" The playfulness apparently over, the boy's tone was a bit wary.

"No," Soren was quick to reassure him. This interlude wouldn't be any fun at all if his wife feared him even a little bit. "I saw you come here and thought you might lose track of time and forget to eat."

"You're right." Taryn stood and glanced around.

"If you are seeking the steadfast Kexen, I sent him off. If he's clever, he'll find his own food. And as we know, he is very clever. Don't worry about him." Soren held out his hand. "As for you, come with me. I have a small surprise."

"Oh?" Taryn said again and put his hand into Soren's. "That is kind of you, your highness."

Soren took the opportunity to kiss the back of his wife's fingers. "You must call me Soren when in informal settings, my dear."

Taryn swallowed visibly. "Soren, then."

Pleased with the small progress, he led Taryn away from the sitting area. When he noticed that the boy still clutched the book, he stopped to tug it from his grasp. Then he put it on the first table he saw and kept going.

Taryn balked. "I wasn't finished with that."

"Someone will bring it to your chambers."

"How do you know that?"

His wife continuing failure to understand his new station in life was endearing. "Dame Edina will know that you were reading it and make sure it gets to you."

"How can you be so sure?"

"Because, my dear, you are—"

"The Duchess of Vostguard," Taryn finished. "Is that really the answer for everything?"

"Pretty much, yes." Soren brought his wife into the inner courtyard through a nearby door that one of the guards opened for them. He was surprised how much he was looking forward to his simple plans. It was like the heady days of his marriage to Merida. That internal comparison didn't bother him as much as it had a day ago. This marriage could be successful. He simply had to make the effort.

"Where are we going?" It was gratifying that the boy hadn't tried to free his hand and walked by Soren's side without hesitation.

"To the part of the courtyard reserved for the royal family." They walked through the hedgerow that acted as a delineation of that place and he pointed up. "That's the hall that houses our chambers. There's a staircase in the corner, leading directly down here. Only the royal family can use it. You can come here anytime you like without bothering to interact with others."

He could see Sam setting up the meal in the gazebo where all the paths converged, and while he should have headed straight for it, some strong need within him gave him other ideas. Turning abruptly, Soren hemmed his bride in against the high row of hedges. The boy looked at him with wide, questioning eyes.

"I have missed you, my dear." That was all the warning he gave before closing in for a kiss. Taryn stiffened only for a moment before relaxing into the hold. Soren had intended to take only a brief taste, but his wife proved too much of a temptation.

With his tongue roaming Taryn's mouth, Soren moved one hand down to his wife's ass and pushed gently to bring their bodies together. He couldn't hold back a groan as his erect cock pressed against Taryn's hip. Better still, there was an answering hardness leaning into him. His bride was also aroused, and there was no better encouragement than that for a husband. His mind raced to remember the blind spots within the courtyard where he might pleasure them both without the prying eyes of guards or courtiers.

"I find I'm hungry for more than food. I know the perfect spot for privacy." Just when he was about to urge Taryn to go to one, his alone time with his wife came to an abrupt end.

"Papa! Papa!"

Chapter Seven

Whatever annoyance Soren might have felt about his daughters intruding on what had turned into a very entertaining afternoon, it flew off in the wind as he watched his family enjoying luncheon together. The pretty gazebo hadn't seen this kind of joy in many years. He'd tried to entertain the girls there on a few occasions since their mother's death, but it hadn't been the same, and they had all sensed it. Now, however, it was different. For at least this short time eating together, it felt as if his family was whole again, even if it was unconventional. As he sat propped against pillows, eating fruit from a bowl, he allowed himself to take simple pleasure in the way that his daughters were conversing with his new wife.

Lilli, in particular, had kept up a steady stream of anecdotes from her day, peppered with the occasional question. "I got to ride my pony, Sparkles, for a whole hour this morning. Papa says I can get a horse next year if I keep up with my lessons. Do you have a pony, Papa Taryn?" The girls had agreed readily to Taryn's plea for them to be informal with him, but young as she was, Lilli had her own notions of the boy's identity. She wanted another parent, and as he couldn't be her mother, he'd become a second father. The ease with which a child could accept the novel situation was an example that he wished that all would follow.

Margrette tsked. "He's a grown man, Lilli. Men don't ride ponies. They ride horses."

Lilli glared at her sister. "But he's not very big, so I thought maybe he had a pony like me."

Soren managed to hide his smile, but Dame Agnes looked up from her needlepoint and weighed in on his daughter's observation. "Princess Lillibet, we have discussed the inappropriateness of making personal remarks."

Taryn, however, waved away the unintended insult. "It's all right. I am rather small for a man, even among my own people, who tend to be shorter than Moorcondians." He glanced at Soren, and for a moment, there was something in his eyes that spoke of appreciation.

"Maybe you're still growing," Lilli observed before stuffing a bite of sandwich in her mouth. "I am," she continued around her mouthful of food. "Everyone says I'm growing like a weed."

"I suppose that's possible," Taryn remarked after a few seconds. "I might gain some height in the next few years."

Soren liked that idea, picturing how much easier it would be to kiss his wife as he fucked him. Then he realized that such growth was only possible because Taryn was still so young. He felt ancient in comparison, but there was no denying that he'd lain in bed with an adult the previous night. And he would be able to do it again that evening. He wasn't sure he could stand waiting. For a brief moment, he considered coaxing his wife to bed in the afternoon, yet put the idea aside. Taryn had to meet the dowager queen soon and needed to spend the time beforehand in whatever way pleased him the most. Too bad they hadn't yet reached a point in their marriage where lying with his husband was that.

Patience. "Do you like to ride?" he asked.

Taryn nodded. "I do, yes."

"Then I shall have the horse master present you with some mounts for you to choose from."

The boy smiled. "Thank you...Soren." It was obvious it was hard for the boy to use his name. It was good that he had recognized that this was the proper setting to do so and had overcome whatever reluctance there was inside his head.

And Taryn's gratitude was obviously sincere. It gave Soren a warm feeling to gift his wife something. As with the girls and Merida, he wanted to make Taryn happy. It was almost scary how much, given the shortness of their acquaintance. Yet, here he was, determined to give Taryn anything within his power in order to put a smile on his lovely face.

Lilli wasn't done with her conversation. "I have to spend the rest of the afternoon on lessons." She made a face. "What are you going to do, Papa Taryn? I bet you don't have lessons."

Taryn actually chuckled, the carefree moment making him look even more beautiful. Enough so that Soren's heart stuttered unexpectedly in response. "No, I don't. But I did spend time in the library. I love to read and learn. Maybe you will too once it's a choice and not a chore."

Lilli's frown put that idea to bed. "I like being outdoors. And I want to learn to fence."

Taryn turned his gaze toward Soren. "Is that not allowed for girls?" The boy looked genuinely perturbed on Lilli's behalf.

Soren felt the need to comfort his wife as much as he would any of his daughters. "It is. Lilli's mother was excellent with a rapier. Nora and the twins have all taken lessons, but like the horse, it's something Lilli is going to have to wait for." He gave his daughter a brief stern look.

The child looked down at her hands. "Yes, Papa." She got over her chastisement quickly, though. "So what *are* you doing this afternoon, Papa Taryn?" She was like a dog with a bone.

Taryn took in a visibly deep breath and let it out slowly. "I've been invited to take tea with the dowager queen."

Lilli bounced with excitement in a way that had Dame Agnes shaking her head. "Oh, tea with Great Grandmamma? That's ever so much fun. I hope you have the little cakes with pink frosting. They're my favorite."

"That does sound delicious," Taryn allowed. He took in another deep breath and sat back against a pillow. His gaze took in the courtyard. "It's so beautiful here. So much sunlight."

Lilli squinted up. "Too much sunlight gives you freckles. Isn't that right, Dame Agnes?"

"Yes, your highness."

Taryn still looked up in wonder. "I think freckles are a fair trade for basking in this warmth."

Lilli, as was her wont, was undaunted. "Dame Agnes says no man will want to marry me if I have freckles."

Soren had to stifle a laugh, knowing the woman would have said no such thing. The nurse sighed and shook her head again. "That is *not* what I said, your highness."

Lilli pouted. "Close enough. I guess it doesn't matter for Papa Taryn, because he's already married to Papa. Papa's stuck with him, freckles or not."

Taryn did laugh, taking no offense clearly because he really was a sweet person. He looked at Soren with more softness in his expression than ever before. "I suppose he is."

Soren stared back, letting the heat of his desire show through his gaze enough that Taryn's cheeks pinked. Then, popping a grape in his mouth, he affected a relaxed air, because he was with his daughters, and Nora for one, would probably understand the meaning of his look. "I suppose I am."

* * * *

The walk to the dowager queen's apartments proved easier than any of Taryn's earlier journeys. Given the private nature of the floor, there was no one about other than guards. He had to admit, as well, that his clothing made him feel worthy of being there and on his way to meet the most powerful woman in all Moorcondia. He held his head high and only allowed his nervousness to show in the way he flexed his fingers repeatedly to dispel it. Even the lovely meal he'd shared with Soren and his daughters hadn't eased his worry beyond the time he'd spent with them. If he could have, he would have stayed with Lilli the entire time between then and this tea. The littlest of Soren's daughters was a marvelous distraction, and it was refreshing, too, how she didn't hesitate to state what others worked hard to avoid.

Maybe if the girls hadn't shown up, Soren would have followed through on his threat of finding somewhere outdoors to slake his lust. Or perhaps it was more honest to say it had been a promise. Try as he might, Taryn couldn't resist the man's advances. A mere look was already enough to send Taryn's blood straight to that place he'd been trying to ignore for years. His desire for other men might be unnatural, but there was no denying how powerful it was, doubly so now that he had permission to accept it. With time, he might come to see this sudden marriage as a blessing. For the moment, however, he needed to worry about passing inspection with Dowager Queen Margrette.

Kexen ushered him to a set of wide doors, flanked by soldiers who appeared oddly different until Taryn realized that they were women. "The Duchess of Vostguard is here for her audience with the dowager queen." The boy could turn on a haughty demeanor with impressive ease. If he found the guards intimidating, he hid it well.

There was no problem, in any event. One of the women turned to open the door and stood aside for Taryn to enter. She then bellowed out his name and title in its full glory before shutting him in. Thank the gods, Kexen was still with him. The groomer had assured him that until he created a circle of ladies in waiting for himself—a thing almost certainly never to happen as far as Taryn was concerned—it was acceptable for Kexen to attend him, no matter where he went or what he did. There was comfort in the familiar, even when it had been unfamiliar only a day prior.

The queen's sitting room was much larger than his own, as it should be, and populated by opulent furniture and elegant ladies of all ages. They watched him discreetly as he walked to the opposite end where Queen Margrette sat on a large settee, then turned their attention back to their needlework or reading. A few were even painting by the light of the large windows on one side, and someone was playing what he now knew was a called a spinet. Unlike at the banquet, this music was slow and soothing. The entire room conveyed a place of comfort rather than the loftiness of the king's reception room. It put him somewhat at ease.

Kexen must have peeled away from him because when he arrived at his destination, he found himself alone. The queen was decked out in brocaded red and gold, with a wimple framing her lined face. She stared at him with her hands sitting on her lap and gave the impression that she could hold that position forever if she wanted. Taryn gave his unique form of greeting to the elderly woman from some distance, unsure of how near to her he was supposed to get.

"Come closer, child. I want a better look at you, and you can't have tea so far away from the table."

Taryn did as he'd been told, and when the woman gestured toward the chair to her right, he understood he was expected to sit. He was careful to keep his knees together as Kexen had taught him. Female clothing and decorum existed with different rules than he was used to, and he didn't want to give offense.

The queen cocked her head to one side as she stared unabashedly at him. "You're younger than I expected—and more male, too." Her wry tone and quick smile put Taryn more at ease.

"Yes, your majesty. I believe everyone is still getting used to the idea that I am a boy bride…myself included."

His response seemed to please the woman, because she smiled broadly before gesturing toward one of her maids. "Have you had tea before?" she asked as the cups were poured.

"No, ma'am. I'm told it's very nice, however, and I'm anxious to try it." His gaze slid to the enormous tray of food sitting on the table to one side. "And there are little cakes with pink frosting. I'm told they are delicious."

The queen barked out a laugh, dispelling her haughty appearance. "That nugget of information surely came from Lilli."

"Yes, ma'am. She said I must try one."

"And so you shall. But first, do you want lemon or milk and sugar in your tea?"

"I'm sorry, but I don't know what to say. Would you be so kind as to recommend which one?"

That answer earned him an approving nod. The queen spoke to her maid. "The duchess will take it with milk and one sugar." She returned her attention to Taryn. "How do you get along with Soren's girls?"

"Well, I believe." He thanked the maid as she handed him his cup and saucer, then took a sip. "Oh, that's lovely." He had no trouble saying those words, because they were true.

She peered at him before giving a nod. "You're honest as well as polite—hardly the savage many were worried about when it was announced that Soren would marry a Marsher."

Taryn felt his cheeks warm, and he stared at his cup. "I can't assure you that I am *not* that. Though there is a lot about your society that I don't understand."

The queen drank some of her tea. "But you're a quick study and appreciative of all that's being done for you. That's what is being said."

Taryn couldn't look her in the eye. "Oh? Am I being talked about? I wouldn't have thought I was a very interesting topic."

The queen laughed. "Oh, my darling boy, people have been talking about little else since you arrived. Not all of it is kind, I will confess, but I listen to the downstairs folk more than the nobility. You are liked where it counts."

Taryn had nothing to say to that, so he concentrated on his tea and turned his attention to a small plate laid down by a maid on a round table by his chair. It was piled with small, thin squares of sandwiches. "This can't all be for me?" The question popped out before he could stop it.

"A sampling of my favorites. Eat what you like and leave the rest. You can even have cake first. I run a very informal salon."

Taryn wasn't sure what the woman meant, but nothing about this room or the people in it struck him as being a casual gathering. He took the topmost sandwich and bit it in two. He'd never had anything like it, some kind of crispy vegetable mixed with a soft cheese. "Delicious," he declared after swallowing the bite.

"I'm gratified you like it. I know how hard it can be to adjust to new foods." She was quiet for a while as Taryn ate and she sipped at her tea. Then, "How is my grandson treating you?"

An image of Soren looming over him as he'd filled him the night before caused him to choke on his next mouthful. Clearing his throat, he said, "Excuse me. I swallowed wrong." The queen's answering grin told him she knew what he'd been thinking of. *No, impossible.* He drained his cup and put it down on the table. "He's treating me very well, ma'am. Prince Soren is a kind and honorable man." His words were accurate, even if he had others he'd like to use as well.

The queen handed her cup to one of the maids and sat back on her settee. "I agree with your assessment of my grandson's character, but he is a soldier at heart, still mourning the loss of his first wife and can't truly understand what all this is like for you."

Taryn wasn't sure how much he should say to this woman. She was, at the end of the day, no matter how sympathetic she might appear, Soren's relative and inclined to see his side of matters. He busied himself with eating another sandwich, this one made of some kind of fish paste that he didn't care for, yet ate anyway. "He's doing his best to be patient with me."

"That has the ring of truth to it, and I expected no less. I would only ask that you be equally patient with him."

That comment surprised him. It was a given that Taryn would have to be the one to bend to Soren's will. He supposed he hadn't been all that kind to his husband and appreciative of how hard this might be on him as well. "Thank you, ma'am. That is sound advice."

"Giving advice is about all I'm good for these days. I'll have a lemon tart," she said to one of the serving maids. "The duchess, I'm sure, would love to try the pink cake now."

Taryn was happy for the dessert, and Lilli had been right about how delicious it was. He wondered what it said about him that his tastes ran along those of a young child. It was nice to eat in companionable silence for a little while, the music washing over him, the subtle sounds of the ladies around him giving the event a homey feel.

"I was a treaty bride too, you know?"

Taryn blinked at the queen in surprise. "No, ma'am, I didn't."

"It was long ago, of course." She got a faraway look in her eyes. "I was a little younger than you are and scared and resentful in equal measure." Her frankness surprised Taryn, and he found himself hanging on her words with keen interest. "I come from Sardinus, a coastal city-state, and brought seafood and a direct trade route for silk. I was very valuable." There was no hint of bitterness in her statement, yet Taryn heard it, nevertheless. "And I loathed my new husband's touch."

The queen finished her pastry and handed the plate back to her maid in exchange for more tea. "There was no surprise there—not on my part, anyway. I'd known for a long time that I didn't want a man, but I also knew that no one would care what I wanted. I was a commodity as much as the fish and the silk." She gave Taryn a wry grin. "Such is the destiny of those born into powerful families. I expect your father didn't ask if you wanted to marry Soren."

"No, ma'am."

"No." She sighed. "The treaty is what matters, the good of your people. I understood that myself, but I couldn't pretend to like my husband's attentions. Fortune smiled upon me, however, as Morlen was a kind man and surprisingly understanding. We came to an arrangement whereby I gave him his heir, and that was that." She sighed and a look of sorrow crossed her face. "Of course, I gave birth to twins — a common event in both our families. The firstborn didn't survive more than a few hours. But our second son, whom we named Soren, as it happens, was a hardy boy who grew big and strong. With the succession secure, my duty had ended. Morlen and I went our separate ways, passion-wise, and became great friends. The only solace I had when the avian plague took my Soren and his queen, was that Morlen hadn't lived to see the loss of our second son."

"I'm sorry," Taryn said quietly. "It must be very hard to lose both your children."

"Very," Margrette agreed. "But there are my grandsons and their children to ease the pain. Soren the Younger's daughters delight me with their frequent visits, and Nora will be an excellent successor to her father's duchy. You haven't met the rest of my grandchildren because Auden's sons are away at university, and little Gracia remains in the nursery. They, too, bring me joy in my later years and bode well for the future of Moorcondia."

Nora had told Taryn this during the banquet, so it wasn't news to him, and he was grateful to have fewer people to interact with at the moment. Nevertheless, he said, "I look forward to meeting the crown prince and his siblings. And Soren and his daughters speak with great affection for you, ma'am."

"A little cake goes a long way in making people like me." She grinned before adding, "And I'm able to be a happy woman because of Morlen's understanding of my nature. He gave me the freedom to find the love of my life." The queen craned her neck to look over her right shoulder. Taryn followed her gaze and noticed for the first time that an even older woman sat on a window seat piled high with pillows. Even so, he could tell that she was tall and broad. She looked to be dozing. "Didn't I, Elspeth?"

The woman startled awake and grimaced at the queen. "What?"

"After I gave Morlen his heir, I was able to find my one true love."

The older woman batted her hand at the queen. "I'd already set my sights on you, silly chit. I would have had you no matter how Morlen felt about it. As good as I was with a blade, no man would have stopped me." With that, the woman closed her eyes again.

The queen looked at Taryn. "Don't be so shocked, boy. You'll find that one of the benefits of being as old as Elspeth and I are is that you can say what you like."

Taryn swallowed hard and tried not to be so wide-eyed. "Yes, ma'am."

She leaned closer to him. "Do you like Soren's touch?"

Taryn stared back at her, tempted to lie. But after what she'd just shared, he felt compelled to tell her the truth. "Yes, ma'am."

"Then that's all that matters, and you are more fortunate than most in that regard. Many are unhappy in that aspect of their marriage, men and women alike. It is a gift that you are attracted to your husband. Don't let anyone tell you differently. People like us have little say in how our lives are going to play out. The least we can do for ourselves is face our own desires head-on and find happiness where we can."

* * * *

The queen's words echoed in Taryn's head as he lay under his husband, Soren thrusting deeply into him with slow strokes. The man's tongue tickled the side of his neck, sending even more shudders through him. As with the night before, Soren had sucked him dry before breaching him. It didn't hurt—quite the opposite, which still stunned him. Climaxing from the blow job had left everything surprisingly lax, pliable and biddable. It was as if his hole welcomed the intrusion, and once Soren's cock was inside Taryn's ass, it brushed some spot he hadn't known existed. The sparks of pleasure were irresistible. He'd hardened again within seconds of being mounted and rode the familiar wave of an orgasm. This was nothing like his own furtive efforts. Soren commanded his body to respond. The climax rose and crashed, tossing him in the air and whirling him about until he collapsed into his mattress, gasping for breath. Now boneless, he could only hold on to his husband and ride out the man's orgasm in turn.

Soren thrust hard and groaned. Warmth splashed inside Taryn, except this time, he didn't mind it. There was even a certain sense of satisfaction that he'd pleased his husband. The part of him that wanted to deny this pleasure and deride it as unnatural and wrong was drowned out by the queen's advice and Soren's obvious appreciation. With the last pulse of his dick, Soren collapsed onto Taryn, his arms keeping his full weight off. Taryn didn't mind. In fact, he hugged his husband tightly to urge him to fully relax.

"I shall crush you, my dear."

"No, you won't. I'm fine." He ran the fingers of one hand down Soren's sweaty back. "You do all the work. That doesn't seem fair."

Soren lifted his head to grin at him. "Any time you'd like to try riding me, I'm happy to accommodate." He kissed him, then, ending any discussion for a while.

"How does that work, exactly?" Taryn managed to ask when Soren finally let him up for air.

Soren brushed Taryn's hair from his face. "Well, I lie on my back, and you sit on my —"

"I get the picture. Thank you." Taryn knew he was blushing. This having sex was still not something he was used to. He wasn't sure he could ever be as open about it as others were.

"You are *adorable*."

Taryn frowned. "I'm not sure I like being called that."

"Why not?"

"It makes me feel young."

Soren peppered his chin with kisses. "You are young, but I try not to think about that. It makes me feel as if I've robbed the cradle."

"You're not old."

"I'm thirty-five."

"Oh, then I take it back. You *are* old." Taryn popped his eyes, wondering how he dared tease his princely husband, a man he barely knew.

But Soren merely laughed, then kissed him again before disengaging their bodies and leaving the bed. Taryn settled into it, waiting for his husband to return with a wet cloth. The previous night, he'd been embarrassed by the treatment. This night, he appreciated the gesture and lay still while Soren cleaned him.

"I meant to ask you earlier how tea with my grandmother went."

Taryn lifted one leg to help give Soren access to his inner thighs. "It was very nice. Lilli was right about the pink cake."

"She always is when it comes to sweets."

Taryn lowered his legs and moved over to allow Soren to slide in beside him. When his husband tugged him into his arms, Taryn didn't resist. This cuddling was rather nice, actually. "The queen was very kind, very sympathetic." He chose his words carefully so as not to be insulting. Soren couldn't help the circumstances any more than Taryn.

"She understands how you are feeling better than anyone, I dare say. Did you meet the formidable Elspeth?"

"Not formally. I think she might be the oldest person I've ever seen."

"I expect she might be, within the palace. Don't be fooled by her age, however. She could slip a knife between your ribs in a flash if you dared to threaten Margrette. Elspeth was a palace guard when they met—middle-aged I believe."

"And no one in your family cares?" It was hard to believe that something he'd been taught his whole life was wrong could be accepted easily.

"My grandparents were happy, and that's all that matters to us. Plus, having met her, who do you think would dare openly scorn her life?" That was true. Margrette was not one to cross. Soren changed the subject. "I've told Rolf to have the horse master ready to meet you in the morning."

"Thank you. I appreciate it. Oh, but I'm meeting with Nora after breakfast to go over my finances."

"The horse master will wait on your schedule, my dear."

"So I am told about mostly everyone. I am eager to pick out a mount and go riding, though." He didn't add that he was also keen to see how much money he had. He hoped to be able to buy Soren a wedding ring. But that was something he wanted to keep as a surprise, which in itself was a surprise to him. In quick order, he'd come to view his husband as more of an ally than a foe. If they both tried, their marriage could work.

"Be careful." Soren's tone was oddly stern.

"Please don't worry. I am a very good rider."

"Nevertheless…" Soren left it that.

Soon Taryn felt the tug of sleep and didn't hesitate to fall into it within his husband's embrace.

* * * *

"That number can't be right."

Nora sniffed. "I assure you it is. I'm very good with figures."

Taryn stared at the ledger some more. "But it's a fortune."

"Certainly. There are few within the palace with one that rivals yours. Myself being one of them, but then I am already a duchess in my own right and will be again when my father passes. Not that his death will affect your income… It's yours by law for the rest of your life."

Taryn sat back and worked to accept the reality of his new station. With the speed in which his circumstances had changed, he hadn't had time to fully appreciate what it meant. He was a wealthy man with money at his disposal that would make a world of difference to his people if he could use it for their betterment. But he knew that was impossible. His father and brother would rather let their people starve than allow him such power.

"Well, at least I can stop worrying about how much my new wardrobe costs. I can afford a lot of silk and velvet with this money, I imagine."

Nora looked at him with shock. "*You* don't pay for your clothing. My father does."

"But why?" He pointed at the ledger. "I can afford to buy them myself. Soren can spend his money on other things."

Nora folded her hands on top of her desk and stared hard at him. "An honorable man sees to the needs of his wife and children. It makes no difference how much money they may have themselves. People will judge him by the condition of his family. If word got out, and it would, that you paid for your own clothing, it would shame him terribly. You don't want that, do you?" she asked suspiciously.

"No! Of course, I don't." Taryn took in then huffed out a deep breath. "Everything is so different now. No one has told me your customs. It seems that I can do or say the wrong thing at any time without knowing it."

Nora gave him a sympathetic smile. "I understand. We all do and will help you as much as you need. You only have to ask."

"All right, then. Is it permissible for me to spend my money on gifts for Soren?"

"Absolutely. Only, you need to pay in coin, otherwise the chits will be sent to my father." Nora rose and went to a domed chest on a nearby shelf. She pulled out a small leather purse and returned to her desk. "Here. This should be enough to serve you for a while, and if you need more, you simply ask."

Taryn opened the purse and peered inside. He tried not to gasp at the shiny abundance. Pulling the strings shut again, he looked at Nora. "What if I ask for too much?"

The girl laughed. "I don't think that's likely."

"I suppose not. Thank you. You've been very kind." He rose and went to shake out his skirts, a gesture that had become ingrained in only a week, except there was little there to manage. He was going riding this morning and that allowed for a shorter, belted kirtle, more like a man's tunic, as well as tight trousers in soft leather.

Nora also stood. "It is truly my pleasure, but I must also say that my sisters and I are pleased by how happy our father seems. He took our mother's death very hard, and we were skeptical that this marriage would make his life better. I'm glad we were wrong."

A bit stunned at this assessment, Taryn struggled for a response. "I am as well."

He took his leave and found Kexen waiting for him in the hallway, flirting with the guards — or trying to, anyway. The stone-faced men seemed immune to the distraction. The boy didn't hesitate, however, to fall in behind Taryn as he walked. The presence of his official groomer felt more like having a friend for the first time in his life. It was a comfort.

"Is there a palace jeweler?"

"There is, your grace, although his shop is nearby in the city."

"Do you think we can pay him a visit before meeting the horse master?" A quick learner, Taryn answered his own question. "Of course we can. The man waits on my schedule, does he not, even if he doesn't know I'm coming?"

"Yes, your grace."

Taryn stopped and faced Kexen. "I want to buy my husband a wedding band. I'm not sure what he would like, though."

The boy looked at his feet for a few seconds. "Platinum, definitely. And men are favoring an inlay of black onyx. It's a gemstone and very masculine."

"That sounds perfect." Taryn opened the purse and held it out for Kexen to see. "Is this enough, do you think, to pay for one?" He felt like the bumpkin that he was, but Nora had been right when she'd said he should ask.

Kexen's eyes widened. "Your grace, that's enough to buy an entire village. So…yes."

Pleased, Taryn closed the purse and tucked it into his belt. "Then let's go. I am keen to order the ring, but I also can't wait to ride."

* * * *

Taryn stared at the three lovely mares that the horse master had lined up for his inspection outside the barn. "They are all quite beautiful." He ran his hand down the neck of one, and she shook her head and snorted delicately. "Perfect for a leisurely ride." His heart sank a little. He'd been expecting something with more spirit.

The horse master stood with legs braced and hands clasped behind his back. "They're the best of his highness' stock. Excellent mounts for a lady."

Taryn's disappointment made him bolder than he wanted. "But I'm *not* a lady."

The man's face turned red. "Of course not, your grace." He bowed low, giving Taryn an unobstructed view of the paddock behind him.

A chestnut-colored horse with a dark mane trotted around it. Intrigued, Taryn went to the fence to get a closer look. He leaned on the upper railing and watched as the frisky creature made the circuit of its confinement before heading toward him. When Taryn dared to reach out and touch its forelock, the horse didn't shy away.

"There now," he crooned. "Aren't you a sight to behold? I bet you hate being boxed in like this." The horse tossed its head, as if in agreement. "I know how you feel." He stroked the horse's neck and patted it gently. "What about this one, Sir George?" Taryn didn't bother to look over his shoulder at the horse master. At this point, he already assumed people were paying attention to him, even when he wasn't focused on them.

The horse master cleared his throat as he joined him. "That's a, ah, gelding, your grace."

Taryn glanced at the man. "I am aware of that. Is he someone's mount?"

"Not at the moment, no." It clearly pained the man to say so.

"Then I'll ride this one."

Now the man grimaced. "Wind Chaser is a bit hard to handle, your grace."

"Good. I like a challenge. Please tack him up." He would have liked to do it himself but knew without asking that it would make the horse master apoplectic. He turned to grin at Kexen. "I can't wait to get out there. I assume you know where we can really give our horses their head?"

"Yes, your grace."

Because Kexen wasn't his usual effusive self, Taryn realized he'd never asked his groomer something. "You can ride, can't you?"

"Very well, your grace."

"Then let's pick out your mount." He raised his face to the sunshine. "It's a glorious day for a ride."

With so many stable hands to ready their horses, it didn't take long before Taryn was cantering away from the walls of the back of the city. The surrounding pastures were flatter than he'd expected and magnificent with their varied colorful flowers sprouting from the greenest grass he'd ever seen. Never in his life had he been able to ride in such an open area, without having to look over his shoulder for trouble following him. After an initial test, Wind Chaser had accepted Taryn's mastery of him and reacted beautifully to every subtle command. Taryn felt in control enough to want to really ride.

"Let's see what you've got, Wind Chaser." He kicked the horse into a gallop and flew across the meadow.

For a short while, Taryn felt free in a way that he never had before, even when he spotted two riders heading straight for him. He slowed his horse in reaction, his heart stuttering with a bit of trepidation until he recognized that it was Soren and Rolf. He came to a stop and raised his hand in greeting, happy to see that his husband might be joining him. That feeling died in an instant as Soren raced to a stop right in front of him, the man's great war horse rearing up with the sudden movement. Taryn worked to keep Wind Chaser under control in the commotion. But that wasn't the problem. What truly made Taryn quiver with familiar fear was his husband's furious expression.

Taryn knew that look from his father and brother, and it always preceded a beating.

Grabbing Taryn's reins in his fist, Soren leaned into him to shout, "What in all the gods do you think you're doing?"

Chapter Eight

Taryn kept his feelings in check until he reached the privacy of his sitting room. Even then, he refused to let his threatening tears come out. Old habits of hiding his fear and embarrassment had served him well as Soren had led him back to the stables then ordered him to go to his room — as if Taryn were a child. He'd refused to let others see how hurt and angry he felt. His pride might not be worth much, but it was all he had, notwithstanding the enormous wealth that he could lay claim to. And no amount of money in the world would save him from his husband's wrath, regardless.

Taryn knew how the rest of the day would play out. Soren would let him wait a long time for his punishment to allow the fear and uncertainty to grow. And what would it be, his hand or a belt? Taryn was well used to both, and he knew that whatever Soren did, it would be hidden from others. Hogard and Hobart hadn't cared if people saw their handiwork, but the more *civilized* Moorcondians likely wanted the violence hidden. Taryn would be forced to spend the evening pretending he wasn't in pain. Well, he could do that to for the sake of his own pride. It had been his life for a long time.

Taryn paced his sitting room, holding himself together. Kexen hovered nearby, having said nothing on the journey back. The poor groomer looked miserable, as if he were somehow to blame. And maybe Soren saw it that way, too. Taryn could only hope that Soren wouldn't mete out punishment for Kexen as well. Taryn had been so enamored of Wind Chaser that nothing Kexen could have said would have dissuaded him from riding the gelding. Guilt ate at him because he knew he was powerless to protect the boy.

"I'm sorry, your grace." Kexen's voice was shaking. "I should have known better."

Taryn stopped and faced him. "This is not your fault. I picked the horse and the ride."

The boy wrung his hands. "But I knew something that you didn't." He swallowed visibly and his eyes shined with unshed tears. "The duke's first wife, Duchess Merida, died when her horse stumbled on a gallop. It crushed her when they fell."

Taryn froze at the news, opening his mouth, then shutting it again when he realized he didn't know what to say. His mind conjured up Soren's expression when he'd ridden up. Had that been fury or fear in his face? Taryn had been going very fast, something he was comfortable doing, but what had Soren seen—an out-of-control horse, perhaps? It had to have conjured up horrible memories of his first wife's death. Taryn didn't have long to ponder the situation further. His door flung open, and Soren strode in.

The man flicked his gaze at Kexen. "Get. Out."

Flashing Taryn a sympathetic look, the boy hurried to do as he'd been told, shutting the door behind him. Taryn took a step forward to tell Soren he was sorry if he'd scared him, even though he worried that it might be an insulting misinterpretation of what had happened. He didn't get the chance. Soren was on him in the next second, reaching for his face. Taryn couldn't help flinching, surprised that his husband was going to inflict visible damage.

But there was no blow. Instead, Soren pulled him in for a bruising kiss that nevertheless sparked a response in Taryn's own body. The next thing he knew, he was bent over the back of one of the beautiful, silk sofas, Soren shoving his tunic up his back. The man had the laces of Taryn's trousers undone in the next instant, exposing his ass. There was a spitting sound, then a wet finger breached his hole. He made himself to relax, because he knew what was coming. Soren's cock was forced into Taryn's ass with burning speed. That pain faded with each thrust, and it ended quickly with Soren shouting out his release. Taryn's came right on its heel. He held on to the sofa with clenched fingers as his orgasm shuddered through him.

For long seconds, there was nothing except their harsh breathing. Soren was still embedded in him, and he gripped Taryn's hips sufficiently hard to leave marks. When it became clear that Soren was in no hurry to say or do anything more, Taryn couldn't help himself. Looking over his shoulder, he asked, "Do you feel better now?"

* * * *

"Do you feel better now?"

Soren had yet to answer his husband's question. When he'd deemed himself under control, he'd disengaged his cock from his wife's ass and carried the boy into the bathing chamber. He'd disrobed him as gently as he knew how before drawing a bath. Of course, he could have called Kexen in to see to the chore. It was the groomer's job. But those who hovered out in the hall had no doubt heard all, and Soren had embarrassed his bride enough for one day. He dumped some flowery gunk into the water before helping Taryn into it. The boy sunk up to his neck, lying against the sloped end. He looked at the wall, not at Soren, obviously not intending to initiate any more conversation on what had happened.

Soren understood that he was the one who needed to make the next move to repair the damage to his marriage. It was hard, though, and he was dirty himself and smelled like horse and the remnants of the fucking. He left to make himself more presentable, washing quickly and donning loose silk trousers. When he returned, Taryn hadn't moved. With an inward sigh, Soren sat on the edge of the bathing tub.

Being a soldier, he tackled the problem head on regardless of how hard it was. "Merida sat a horse as well as any soldier, and she loved galloping across meadows and cantering through forests. She was fearless and so competent that I never thought to worry. I was training with my men, laughing over how I'd dumped one into a horse trough, when the captain of the palace guard came to me with the news of what had happened to her. I'd known that man my whole life. A more stoic person you'd never meet and yet there were tears in his eyes."

The memory hit him hard as if fresh, but he pushed past that pain. "Her horse had stumbled in a hidden animal burrow. It went down on its side, crushing her beneath. I was told that she died almost instantly. *Almost.*" He couldn't help wondering, as he'd often done before, if she'd known even for a few seconds that her life was over. "It was shocking in its unexpectedness, as all accidents are, I suppose. But we'd survived the avian plague, she, the children and me. After months of worry and grief over my parents' death, I think my guard was down.

"Telling my girls was the hardest thing I've ever had to do. I would go into battle a thousand times over rather than having to tell my sweet darlings that their mother was gone." He lowered his head. "I think I went a little mad for a while. Nora was the one who lent me her strength and helped me pick myself up. It took a while for me to allow the girls to ride again themselves. It's hard to let go of the worry. Lilli should already have progressed beyond her sedate pony to a more spirited horse. I'm the one who needs that extra year, not her."

Soren went silent then, even as he knew he should tie that past with the present situation more precisely. But he kept seeing Taryn flying across that field and picturing him going down as Merida had done. A hand landed tentatively on his thigh. He raised his head to see Taryn staring at him with tears pooling in his eyes.

"I'm so sorry, Soren. I didn't know, and even if I had, I can't promise I would have linked my riding and her death. You loved her, so it was natural for you to grieve her. I'm just someone you were forced to marry — and a substitute bride at that."

Soren leaned over to brush away a tear that had slipped down Taryn's cheek before taking Taryn's hand and kissing the back of it. "You don't value yourself enough, my dear. The last thing I want is for you to die, and it has nothing to do with the damn treaty."

Taryn dropped his gaze. "I'm glad to hear it. You've been a better husband than I could have ever hoped for. I'm sorry that I was difficult in the beginning."

"You were scared and resentful," Soren hastened to point out. He didn't want his bride to feel guilty about anything. "And I hurt you — the night we wed and this afternoon." The compulsion to mount his wife had been frightening in its intensity. He'd been out of control — and that was not something he was used to.

"You didn't hurt me just now. I was expecting a beating, so an orgasm was a welcome surprise."

Soren was furious all over again at Taryn's family for how they'd abused him, but more at himself. "I would *never* lay a hand on you that way." He swallowed back the bile threatening to spill out. "There is no excuse for how I treated you. I am very sorry."

"I understand why you did it. You were looking to control me in some way, to keep me safe, as it happens. And to vent your *emotions*."

"That's both true and not an excuse."

Taryn licked his lips and sat up. "Maybe we can agree to avoid reasons for apologizing to each other. I'm beginning to appreciate that our marriage could be a good one if we try — if you want to," he added with a shy smile.

Soren kissed his wife's hand again and held it to his chest. "I do. Very much so." He breathed deeply. "And to that end, if you want Wind Chaser, he is yours. You ride well. I could tell even through my haze of fear and fury. *But*, we ride together. I promise that we'll do more than a pokey walk around the meadow. I just need to see you for myself when you let that horse fly as magnificently as he does."

Taryn smiled broadly. "I think that's an excellent idea."

It was a simple as that. They had found a way forward, and sitting there, holding his wife's hand and becoming aroused at the sight of his glistening skin, Soren knew that their lives together would be wonderful.

* * * *

"So you're sure that my becoming a patron of the library won't insult the king?"

Soren used his grip on his wife's hand to bring him closer. He liked touching Taryn and didn't care one wit that such open affection was unusual in the palace. Let the denizens of his brother's court make of it what they would. The last month had seen a delightful evolution of his marriage, from political to affectionate. The way things were building between them, Soren had high hopes that theirs could yet be a love match — at least on his side of matters. It was hard to know what went on inside Taryn's head, because he was still so guarded. But he was shyly affectionate and becoming more bold in bed. Those were good signs that his Marsher bride was warming to him and their unconventional arrangement.

"I promise you the king won't care in the least. Lots of people are patrons of the library, my grandmother included. Even in a rich country like Moorcondia, there are many demands on the king's coffers. He can't always afford to allocate enough, even for a national treasure such as the library. Besides," he added with a swift kiss of Taryn's hand, "everyone knows how much you love it. You spend as much time there as you do in our chambers."

"That's all right, isn't it?"

Taryn was still wary of him and uncertain of his own place in both society and their marriage. They were getting along so well that it was easy to forget that. "Of course it is, my dear. Your time is mostly yours to spend how you like. And I don't expect you want to play cards with the idyll nobles."

"No, definitely not. Kexen explained the basic concept, and it seems like a waste of time to me."

"Many would agree with you, myself included."

"It's settled, then. I'll let Dame Edina know tomorrow. She will be delighted, I dare say. And I need to spend all that money I have somewhere, given that I'm not allowed to use it for my own needs."

Soren gave him a sideways glance. "Absolutely not. Anything you want is my pleasure to give you." They'd had a brief conversation about that a few weeks back while Soren had been feeling *very* satisfied. Not that his brain had been so mushy as to agree that Taryn should pay for his own clothing, or anything else, for that matter. In this, Soren was very traditional.

"I am permitted to buy gifts, though, am I not?" There was a coyness to his wife's tone.

"You are. Do you have something and someone in mind?"

"It's possible. Perhaps I'll show you after supper a recent purchase that was only completed this morning."

Soren could tell that Taryn was bursting with enthusiasm, and while it was easy to guess that the gift was for him, he played along with the teasing. "I'll be happy to give you my opinion as to whether the recipient will enjoy it."

"Good. I'll be very interested to hear your views." There was a smile in his tone, and he squeezed Soren's hand.

Suddenly, Soren couldn't wait to get his bride alone. "We should both bathe before supper. We stink of horse. We will offend the delicate noses of my royal family." They'd ridden nearly every day for an hour or so since his epic blow-up. It was an enjoyable way to end his day after training, and Taryn loved it so much.

His wife huffed as they entered the palace. "Is decorum the only reason why you want both of us to take a bath?"

"Well…"

"Oh, you're incorrigible. There will be plenty of time for that tonight."

Pleased at how well his wife had accepted what happened in their marriage bed, Soren let the heat show in his eyes. "There is never enough time."

Taryn tsked. "I still have my dance lessons this afternoon. Remember?"

"Yes," Soren replied with a sigh. "You don't have to do that, you know."

"I want to. Kexen says the ball season is the most important of all for the palace and that the royal family always leads off the dance each night. I don't want to embarrass you."

"You could never do that, my dear," Soren said with a chuckle. His good humor died in an instant as he spotted Tost striding toward them with two palace guards in tow. He knew that look on the minister's face, and his stomach dropped at the possible problem being brought to him.

Tost stopped in front of them both, bowed at Soren and threw a glare at Taryn. "Your highness, I have terrible news."

"Get on with it." Soren had no patience for theatrics, especially as he could surmise what was happening.

The man drew himself up to his full height. "The Marshers have broken the treaty."

Although Taryn made no noise, his hand spasmed in Soren's. Soren wanted to reassure his wife, but duty dictated he address the problem first. "How so?"

"They raided a village on the very edge of our border a few days ago. It was completely sacked. No one was spared. A few managed to flee and get to a garrison. A rider arrived a short while ago to tell the king."

"I see. I will go to him now."

"He did send me to find you, your highness." Tost turned his attention to Taryn. "These guards will see to the securing of the duchess."

Now it was Soren's turn to tighten his grip. Then he let it go and spoke directly to his wife. "Go to our chambers and stay there. I will come to you before I have to leave."

Taryn raised his head yet didn't look at him. "Very well."

The control his wife was showing broke Soren's heart. He'd come to learn that Taryn was at his most frightened when he looked indifferent. His instinct to hide his feelings was well-honed. When he was in danger, it kicked in. Soren wanted to reassure him but couldn't take the time and didn't want to have an intimate conversation with Tost and many others within earshot. Already courtiers and nobles were gathering along the hallway. News had spread fast, no doubt, as it always did. Everyone was keen to see how the Marsher duchess would react and be treated.

Because he couldn't give his wife the words of comfort directly, he trained his gaze on the guards. "I will trust you to safely deliver my wife to our chambers. I hold you responsible for him."

The guards nodded curtly, stone-faced but hopefully clever enough to appreciate that he was not one to cross. Then help came in the form of Rolf, gods bless him. The man came rushing to his side.

"The men are making ready, your highness, on the assumption we will march tonight."

Soren clasped him on the arm. "Good man. Accompany the duchess to his room while I confer with the king." He conveyed his worry with his eyes alone, knowing Rolf would pick up on it.

"Yes, your highness." Rolf focused on Taryn and gestured with his hand. "Your grace?"

With admirable composure, Taryn nodded once to Soren, then started walking away. Soren watched him for a few seconds, resisting the urge to go after him and escort him to their chambers himself. Because that was impossible, he turned to Tost instead and got right into the man's face. There was some satisfaction when he flinched.

"Your guards better take care with my wife."

Tost tried to look unperturbed. "The fate of the duchess is not in my hands."

"No," Soren said, remembering his brother's words. "It's in mine. The gods help anyone who thinks otherwise and acts rashly."

Having made his threat clear, Soren strode away, heading for the king's council room, his stomach in knots over the Marshers' perfidy. He knew his duty and would do it without hesitation, but damnation, he had really hoped to be wrong about the treaty being broken. A month ago, it had merely bothered him. Now that he had grown closer to his bride, this outcome was a nightmare come true.

* * * *

Taryn forced himself to walk slowly to his chambers when what he really wanted to do was race there and shut out the rest of the palace. The halls were filled with people, everyone watching him as he was escorted to his prison. Most didn't even bother to hide their sneers and snide remarks. Lady Balter was there, a smug look on her face. No doubt she was already planning how she would greet Soren when he returned victorious. And he would. Hogard had ensured the most extreme response by the Moorcondians with their most wretched act to date. This was far worse than a quick raid. The Moorcondians had no choice now other than to wage a full-out war. The outcome of it was not in doubt. So much so that he wondered how his father and brother could think otherwise. Their stupidity was surprising, even to him.

As he concentrated on putting one foot in front of the other, it felt as if the air were thick and revolting, as if each step required pushing through some unseen yet corporeal miasma. It helped him keep his slow pace, however, as well as his indifferent expression, giving him something other than people to concentrate on. Some of the palace inhabitants, mostly servants, showed pity on their faces as he passed. He wasn't sure what was worse, but he wasn't going to let them see his misery and fear. He wouldn't give them the satisfaction if they hated him or provide them with extra worry if they rooted for him — not that it truly mattered. His fate was sealed regardless. Everyone had to know it.

It got better when they climbed to the next floor, few dwellers being about. That meant he became extra aware of the ringing footsteps of the guards' booted feet behind him. It felt as if his executioners ushered him to his fate, and it wasn't a purely fanciful notion. His chambers would become his prison and maybe the last walls he would see in his life, however much of it was left. When they arrived at his sitting room door, the two palace guards flanked it with stone-faced efficiency. He wasn't fooled by the lack of outward signs of their thoughts. Their hatred of him emanated from them in silent waves.

Ever the gentleman, Rolf opened the door and ushered Taryn inside. "Your grace." He bowed his head.

Taryn took a moment to speak his mind. "Thank you, Sir Rolf. Please look after the prince. This is going to be hard on him, I believe."

"Always, your grace." The man paused. "Please remain inside your rooms. It won't help his highness if he's worried about you."

"I won't give him any trouble." Taryn meant the words. He and his family had caused enough problems for Soren, starting with shoving a boy bride down his throat. If he'd once thought the prince worthy of only Taryn's ire, the past few weeks had changed his mind.

Saying no more, he entered the sitting room and couldn't hold back the wince as the door closed behind him. It was so quiet, and he knew before he even made his way to the bed chamber that he was alone. Disappointment caused his shoulders to droop and the tears he'd been holding back started to leak out. It had been a foolish hope to expect Kexen to provide him with some company and maybe comfort in what was now the darkest hours of his whole miserable life. *He hates me, too.*

No sooner than he'd thought it, he heard footsteps. Kexen raced into the room so quickly that he skidded to an awkward halt when he spied Taryn. The boy's eyes were as moist as Taryn's felt. "Oh, your grace, I'm so very sorry. I was downstairs when I heard the news and tried to get here before you." He took a step closer. "Are you all right?" He answered his own question. "What a stupid thing to ask. Of course, you're not."

Taryn willed his tears away. There was no reason to make Kexen any more miserable than he already was. "It's fine. I'm glad you're here. You took a risk, though, assuming I'd be here instead of the palace dungeons. Does it have any?" It was a ridiculous question, but he was suddenly curious.

Kexen blinked at him a few times. "Beneath the barracks, yes, but you would never end up *there.*"

"No, I don't suppose members of the royal family ever do. Moorcondia is too civilized for that, isn't it?" He managed to flash a smile. "You've been such a good friend to me. Really, the only friend I've ever had." He hated how pathetic he sounded. "It's kind of you to come to me."

Kexen visibly pulled himself together, too. "Where else would I be? You need me now more than ever."

"Thank you." Taryn was humbled by the simple devotion. "I hope you won't get into trouble for your kindness."

Kexen scoffed. "Who would dare do such a thing? I am your loyal servant until you will it otherwise."

Taryn nodded once, as his decision of what came next formed inside his head. There was only one thing, the only thing that he *could* do to show his appreciation for Soren, his daughters, Kexen and all the others who had welcomed him pointlessly into their lives. "Would you please draw me a bath? I'm dirty after my ride." That was the truth, yet not all of it. There was no point in making it difficult for Kexen before it was necessary.

"Certainly, your grace." The boy seemed happy to have something productive to do and hurried into the bathing chamber.

Alone again, Taryn steeled his spine and went back into the sitting room. There, he took the carved bird his mother had given him and the purse with the rest of the coins Nora had handed him a month ago. He hadn't managed to spend it all as he'd predicted. Then, he sat at the delicate writing desk. He was glad he'd been indecisive about how to redecorate the room. It would have been a waste of money, and while Soren was wealthy, it had never sat well with Taryn to spend so much of it. He opened the top right drawer, his heart thudding with the greatest agony so far, and took out the small black box the jeweler had given him. Inside, the shiny ring he'd commissioned for his husband emphasized how foolish he'd been. *It was never going to work.* He'd always known that his father would break the treaty. For his whole life, he'd steeled himself for disappointment and turned away from thoughts of useless hope. Yet for a brief few weeks, living in the sun-kissed land of Moorcondia, he'd let his guard down.

Knowing Soren wouldn't want the ring as a reminder of their doomed marriage, Taryn put the box next to the other two items, the sum total of his valuable possessions. He wrote what he needed to, sticking to practical matters. There was so much in his heart that he wanted to say but trying to would only cause him to cry in earnest and possibly soften his resolve. When he was done, he joined Kexen in the bathing chamber. He let his groomer disrobe him and undo his braid before stepping into the bath and sliding under the water up to his shoulders.

Taryn looked at Kexen. "Thank you. It's the perfect temperature." He had to pause a moment to gather his courage before holding out his hand. "Please give me your knife."

Kexen was already obeying before the import of Taryn's words must have hit him. He paused in the act of drawing it from its scabbard. "Why?" When Taryn simply stared at him, the boy shook his head. "No! No, your grace. You will not do *that*."

Taryn strove for patience, but anger leaked out. "Would you have me make Soren do it himself? Because he would, you know. He's too honorable to leave it to others. I can't do that to him. It took me a while to appreciate his kindness. Now that I have, I can't bear the idea of making him mete out my punishment. It's not fair, and I won't do it! I lo—" He couldn't bring himself to say it all out loud, even though he knew that it was true. Foolish boy that he was, he'd fallen in love with his enemy.

"But, your grace, why are you certain that's your fate? Did the prince say anything when you left him?"

Taryn closed his eyes briefly, an image of Soren's stricken face as they'd parted. "I've read the entire book Dame Edina gave me on the history of this country. I know the fate of treaty brides when their families break them."

"That was long ago!"

"Not so much. The last one was only a couple of generations older than the dowager queen." He glared at Kexen, his emotional reserves at an end. "Give me the knife." He held his hand out and left it there until the boy complied. He gripped it tightly, willing his hand not to shake. "Thank you. Now, please go — not just out of the bathing room, but the entire chambers. I don't want you here to see this."

"You're so keen to die alone, then?"

"I don't want to die at all, but you know what my people did to yours. There will be no quarter given this time. Moorcondia will wipe out the Marsher plague, once and for all."

"You don't know us as well as you think you do, your grace."

Taryn huffed out a laugh. "I haven't had time to, have I?" He forced his expression to be passive. No reason for poor Kexen to be more upset than he already was. "I left what I hope will be a legally sufficient letter, giving you my bird carving and what's left in my purse. I have nothing else of value. And I want whatever other money might have been already allocated to me to be gifted to the library."

Kexen grimaced. "I don't want your money."

"Take it anyway. You have been an excellent groomer, but you are better than that. I hope the money helps you find a good place. Now, please go."

It took a few seconds before Kexen complied, his usual biddable self clearly warring with a side that Taryn had never seen before. When he did leave, it was at a run. A moment later, the outer door shut loudly enough to startle Taryn. The knife nearly slipped from his fingers. Tightening his grip, he held the blade to the inside of his other wrist. His hand did shake, horribly now.

"Don't be a coward. You can do this...for Soren. And for yourself. For once, take hold of your own destiny." Despite his resolve, the shaking increased, forcing him to put his hand on the rim of the tub. He took in a few deep breaths and let them out slowly to settle his nerves. Then he tried again.

* * * *

"I'm still mystified as to why they attacked there." Soren leaned over the map to study the location of the sacked village. "It's remote, I'll grant you, but over here is more so." He pointed to a spot on the other side of the border with the Marshlands. "It would have taken even longer for word to get to us, and they have more ways to retreat."

Even though Soren had been speaking to his brother, Tost ventured forward with a response. "It was closer for them. Easier. The Marshers are a lazy people, your highness."

Soren grimaced but he couldn't really argue the point, not from what he'd seen of Hogard and his odious son. Taryn, however, had shown him a different side of those people, a better and more industrious one. He couldn't let himself think of his wife. The boy had to be terrified of the war to come and being left behind in a place filled with people who saw him as the enemy. Soren would have to steal a moment before leaving to reassure him of his safety and to make sure that it wasn't an empty promise. Tost, for one, was not to be trusted.

"Perhaps," he allowed, letting none of his thoughts to show. "It's still a limited access point. We can box them into that canyon as they flee us."

The king stopped what had been incessant pacing as he issued orders and came to stand beside him. "I think it is a mistake to assume they had any plan at all. Do you think they never intended to abide by the treaty, or did Hogard find courage in his cups to break it?"

Soren opened his mouth to say that he had no idea what went on in that man's head when a commotion in the anteroom caught his attention. He and everyone else turned their heads in the direction of the closed set of doors. There were raised voices, one of which sounded familiar. He racked his brain to place it, even as his heart started pounding.

"What in the name of the gods!" the king roared.

Something clicked in Soren's head. "Rolf, see to it."

The reliable soldier didn't hesitate to comply. He knew what Soren wanted of him and he didn't bother to check if the king was okay with it. Soren's liege man threw open the doors, allowing the voices to ring clear into the council room and the scrum of men to become visible. Slight as he was, Kexen was holding his own against a couple of guards who were trying to carry him backward.

"Let me go! I must speak with Prince Soren. He'll have you whipped if you don't let me." Amid the flailing arms, the boy spotted him. He stuck out his hand. "Your highness, please!"

"Isn't that your wife's personal groomer?" The king sounded almost amused.

Soren wasn't. He rushed to the boy's side. "Put him down!"

The guards complied with his bellowed command, dropping the boy to the floor with a thud. From his crumpled position, Kexen looked up at Soren and didn't even catch his breath. "Go to him, your highness. Hurry. He's in the bath...with a *knife*."

The groomer hadn't finished puffing out his last word before Soren took off at a run. It didn't matter that courtiers and servants scattered at his approach, like startled birds. He barreled through them all, his focus on a single destination. His stomach clenched at the import of Kexen's words and even as he took the stairs two at a time, he feared he would be too late.

"Move!" he yelled at the guards by Taryn's door and flung it open.

Soren knocked furniture over in his haste and stumbled into the bathing room. What he saw there nearly sent him to his knees. Taryn lay in the bath, a knife held loosely in one hand. He looked at Soren with tears streaming down his face. Soren practically crawled over to him, his relief exhausting him and making his muscles weak, as if he'd run halfway across the country. He clapped his hand over Taryn's wrist the moment he was able and held it tightly to make sure that blade didn't get any closer to his wife's vulnerable skin.

"I'm sorry." Taryn's voice was soft and watery. "I don't have the courage to do it. I wanted so much to spare you and be brave about embracing my fate, but I need your help, after all."

Soren dropped on his ass and found the energy to take the knife from Taryn's grip and toss it aside. "Foolish boy, did you think I was going to execute you?"

"You're too honorable to leave it to someone else."

"I would appreciate the compliment if it didn't come with the assumption that I would casually slit your throat before charging off to battle your father. That *was* what you were thinking, was it not?"

Taryn didn't have to answer. Soren knew. "Damn that library. It's filled your head with the worst kind of knowledge, such as a treaty bride is as much a hostage as a wife. Her life is given to guarantee the commitment. Honor the treaty, and she lives. Break it, and the bride is sacrificed. That is what you were expecting."

Taryn nodded. "It's in your history books as proven fact, not fanciful tales."

Soren sighed. "I may have to add reading to the list of things you may not do without me."

"But I already knew it. Everyone does. I just didn't want to think about it. I was scared enough about the marriage. My father has never cared about me. I should have warned you."

Soren reached out slowly to cup Taryn's cheek. "My dear, it was never your responsibility to explain how untrustworthy your father is. I knew. The king and his ministers knew. I expect even the palace washer women did. We hoped it would work out, but...I should have reassured you long ago that the king put your fate in my hands, and there was never any chance of my taking your life."

Taryn leaned into the touch, a good sign of trust, although fine tremors shook his body. "I'm no good to you now."

The simple statement broke Soren's heart. "My darling wife, you have never appreciated your worth."

Mustering his strength, Soren stood and plucked Taryn out of the bath. He cradled his wet bride against his chest, grabbed a towel and did his best to wrap it around Taryn as he brought him into the bedroom. Then he sat on the edge of the bed with the boy on his lap and rubbed him dry. With his blood rushing through his veins as if he'd been in battle, his dick reacted in the predictable way. He did his best to ignore it, but there was no room to keep it from pressing against his wife's enticing and naked rump.

Taryn shuddered. "You want to mount me."

Soren stilled his actions and used one finger to turn his bride's head in his direction. "What I want is to make love to my wife. I always want to do that, but given that I found you in the process of trying to kill yourself, my body is on high alert. For some inexplicable reason, blood tends to rush to a man's cock when he's in fighting mode. And while I would like nothing better than to spend the rest of the day in this bed with you, duty calls."

What Taryn did next was surprising, although it shouldn't have been. He laid his head against Soren's shoulder in a gesture of utter trust then burst into quiet tears. That turned quickly into full-on sobbing, yet still utterly silent. *He's learned to hide his misery, to not disturb others with it.* Each new revelation about his wife's life before their marriage caused Soren's fury at the Marsher chieftain to grow. He would not have wished the current circumstances to have occurred, but now that they had, he looked forward to crushing the man once and for all. He could only hope that Taryn wouldn't hate him for it. Blood was a strange thing. Even a brutal father was still a father and someone hard to let go of.

Soren ignored the part of him that urged speed. The Marshers could wait. He held his wife as he cried and gave what comfort he could. The crying petered out, and Taryn rested limply against him. Soren brushed Taryn's hair from his drying tears and placed a kiss on his temple. "You need sleep." He tucked a compliant Taryn under the covers and kissed him briefly on the lips. When he tried to straighten, however, the boy grabbed him by the arms with unexpected strength.

"Promise you'll be careful."

Soren tried for a reassuring smile. "Always."

"Come back to me. Please."

"That is my plan." A thought occurred to him. "I will make sure of your safety, no matter what. Life is...unpredictable, as you know."

Taryn's eyes widened. "I don't care about myself."

Soren kissed his wife again because he both wanted to and because he didn't want him to see the new rage building within him. "I do," he said when he found the strength to pull away. "Very much. I hate the idea of your being cooped up in our chambers, but this will be the safest place for you. Promise you won't try to leave it."

"I promise. Please don't worry about me. I will do nothing to anger the king."

"Good. Now I will fetch Kexen so that he may look after you." Soren straightened. "He risked his life to get to me. The house of Vostguard owes him a great debt of gratitude."

Tears rose in his wife's eyes again. "He's a loyal friend. I don't deserve him, but I will show him how much I value him every day. I swear."

Soren nodded. Because he wanted so very much to join his wife if only to hold him while he slept, he forced himself to leave abruptly and not look back. Rolf and Kexen were waiting for him in his sitting room. The groomer looked as if he'd been in battle himself—and he had been. It was a minor miracle that he hadn't been killed by the king's guards. The boy had made many *friends* since arriving at the palace, no doubt, and that was what likely saved him. *And Taryn.* Soren didn't care how much trouble his wife had had killing himself. Eventually, he would have succeeded, of that Soren was sure. The thought turned his guts to water as nothing ever had before.

"You still have your head, I see."

Kexen grinned briefly. "Yes, your highness."

"Go to him and stay by his side until I return. Keep him safe." He wanted to say more but there was no time. The boy didn't need to be told twice, racing from the room. Soren turned to Rolf. "I need you to do one more thing before we leave."

"Anything, your highness."

"Those guards out there are Tost's men, told to keep the duchess in, not protect him. They can't be relied upon to keep my wife safe, especially from them. Pick six guards you trust without reservation and have two stand watch, one each outside my door and Taryn's at all times. No one is to be allowed in—*no one*—except Kexen, Deward and my daughters. If the men do their job, they will be rewarded handsomely. If they do not, I will personally separate their heads from their bodies."

Chapter Nine

"Luncheon has arrived, your grace."

Taryn moved from staring out of the window to join Kexen and Deward. The men laid the platter of food on the table where Taryn took his breakfast with his husband each morning. Because he had the run of both chambers, he preferred to spend time where his fondest memories were. It was silly, really, but Soren's scent permeated his rooms, and that helped ease Taryn's incessant worry. And because the serious Deward acted as if it were perfectly within Taryn's rights to do so, he was certain Soren wouldn't mind.

"It smells delicious." Taryn sat in his usual seat and tried to show interest in each dish as Kexen revealed them.

"I'm gratified to hear it, your grace. Perhaps you'll eat some of it instead of pushing it around your plate, pretending to as if you were a child who hates his vegetables." The groomer was already tasting a bit of each.

"You don't really think someone will try to poison me, do you?" When Kexen had first started, Taryn had been genuinely worried for his own safety. He'd promised Soren that he would be careful, and he didn't want to upset his husband on his return by actually dying this time. With a few days of peaceful boredom, however, the idea that someone would try to kill him seemed more ridiculous. He was nothing without Soren, likely already a distant memory for the denizens of the palace.

It was Deward who answered. "Given that I have only trustworthy people cooking for you, no, but Kexen and I agree that we are not taking any chances. The prince expects us to protect you, and that is what we're doing."

Taryn smiled. "I don't deserve either of you."

"Probably not," Kexen replied, while the more formal valet left the table area to swipe at imaginary dust motes. The man's quiet devotion had been surprisingly reassuring. If anyone was a good indicator of how Soren felt about someone, it was his valet, the person who tended to Soren's most intimate needs.

Being effectively imprisoned with Taryn, Kexen was always happy when meals arrived. He filled his own plate and stood by the table eating it. No matter how much Taryn insisted, the boy would not take Soren's old seat.

They ate in companionable silence for a while, and Taryn did force himself to actually put food in his mouth. It was sinful to waste it, and he didn't want Kexen to worry more than he was. "I don't suppose there's any word." His fear for Soren's safety built each day.

Kexen shook his head. "Nothing, but you shouldn't expect there to be. It's going to take a couple of more days to move that many soldiers to their destination. It's at the far most reaches of our borders. We probably won't hear anything until days after whatever battle ends up being waged. And if our people push through into the Marshlands…" He shrugged. "We have to prepare for weeks of knowing nothing."

Taryn knew this already, yet still felt compelled to ask. His concern was that great. He couldn't imagine his life now without Soren. Against all expectation, the prince had become the center of his world, his reason for living. It was too hard, as well, to think of how his husband would probably invade the Marshlands, all hope of a treaty gone with his father's perfidy. Taryn could only hope that Soren would show mercy to the people who had had no choice but to obey their chieftain. He chided himself for even doubting it, but Hogard had provoked a war in the worst possible way. Tempers were running high, and angry men with their blood up from battle were hard to control.

"I have to trust him."

Kexen cocked his head. "Your grace?"

"Nothing. Just thinking out loud."

There was a knock on the door, and Deward went to see to it. Since Taryn had been imprisoned in his gilded cage, Soren's daughters had visited once a day but usually later in the afternoon. Curious, he stood and met the valet halfway across the room. The man held a wooden tube of some sort.

"What's that?"

Kexen hurried to join them. "A map. I had it brought from the library. I thought it might help if you could see where Prince Soren was going."

Taryn grinned. "Brilliant."

Kexen took the tube from Deward and went to Soren's desk. Then he shook the map out to lay it flat. Taryn felt ill at ease, imposing on Soren's personal space, but when he saw how big the piece of paper was, he could appreciate that it needed more space than his own dainty writing desk would provide. Besides, Deward said nothing about it and even joined them to stare at it.

Kexen used various objects to weigh the corners down and put his finger on the map. "This is the palace. And the prince will be marching his men along this route, in all likelihood. It's the only one that makes sense, given how many of them there are. Plus, there are enough towns along the way to get provisions if a need arises."

Leaning over the desk, Taryn studied it eagerly, following Kexen's finger until it stopped. "I can see now how far away it is." That was also the case for the Marshers. Why had his father not picked a closer location to raid? He studied the map more closely. "Are those mountains?"

"Small ones, yes. They're called the Faerie Hills. No one knows why—or at least that's what I've heard. It's harsh country, very rocky, not good for farming. There aren't many villages that way. None now, I guess," he added in a quiet voice.

But Taryn could barely hear the boy because something screamed inside his head. He'd heard that name before—or something like it. "Faerie Hills? Not Faerie Canyon?" He put his nose practically into the map to see the images there.

"There is a canyon, yes. Here." Kexen moved his finger to a spot where a thin trail lay between two hills not quite as tall as the mountains around them. "It's said to have been carved from the rock by a long-ago river."

Taryn closed his eyes and the room spun as the information flooded in. He staggered to a nearby chair and sat heavily. Kexen and Deward were both by his side in a flash, their hands out to steady him. "I've heard my father and brother speak of it before. They always talked freely around me, as if I weren't there." He stared up at each of the servants in turn. "That same water carved tunnels and caves through the rocky hills that flank it. Hobart found them while on a reconnaissance mission to locate new pickings for his raids. They lead up to the cliff top.

"The Marshers will be able to lay in wait for them above, and we're good archers. Even if we weren't, it will be easy to rain so many arrows down that Soren and his men will be massacred." He grabbed Kexen's arm. "It's a trap."

* * * *

Taryn stopped his pacing when Nora came sailing into the room. The young woman wore an expression that caused his stomach to drop. "No luck?"

Nora shook her head. "I couldn't even glimpse the king, let alone talk to him, before Tost sent me away."

Deward had fetched Nora as quickly as he could, it being agreed that she was the only one who stood a chance of getting news to the king. Tost had threatened to flay Kexen alive if he caught the boy approaching the king's council room again, and they had believed the threat. There was no point in risking Kexen's life for an effort that was doomed to fail. The older, less threatening yet also less well-connected Deward would never get past the first layer of guards. It seemed logical that the king's niece would fare better.

Taryn didn't try to hide his frustration. "What did he say when you warned him of the trap?"

Nora grimaced. "That nothing coming out of your mouth could be trusted. I'm sorry," she added, clearly upset, reminding him that her father's life was on the line. "And Great Grandmamma has left for her country house. She hates when we are at war and always leaves the palace to shut out the endless gossip about it. There is no one else who can outflank Tost."

"The queen?" Taryn ventured. He didn't know the woman well, but she seemed sympathetic.

Nora killed that hope. "My aunt is a lovely person, but she never involves herself in politics."

"Gods!" Feeling defeated, Taryn dropped into a chair and worked to keep his tears at bay. Crying wouldn't help save Soren. He took a few deep breaths and calmed his mind. The obvious answer came to him quickly. "I'll go to him. Soren, that is."

Kexen, Deward and Nora looked at him as if he had two heads. It was the groomer who said the obvious. "Your grace, you are not allowed to go out." He pointed toward the door. "The guards are under orders to protect your life, and that includes not allowing you to leave these chambers."

"We'll have to find a way to get around that problem." He leaned forward as the plan took shape. "A single man riding flat out will make faster ground than all those marching soldiers. You said yourself, Kexen, that they move slowly of necessity. With luck, I'll catch up to them before they enter that canyon." *Please, gods, let me reach him in time.*

Nora pursed her lips. "It could work. I've seen you ride."

"It's certainly a better plan than all of us sitting here and waiting for the prince and his men to be massacred," Deward declared, showing more emotion than Taryn had ever seen before.

Kexen threw up his hands. "First of all—your highness, your grace, *Master* Deward—this plan is risky in the extreme with many points of failure possible. Second, that being said, there will be two riders."

"Are you suggesting you come with me?" Taryn didn't want to put his friend in danger, but the idea of having company was tempting.

"Naturally! I can sit a horse as well as anyone, and I know Moorcondia far better than you. Even if we ride straight through, one horse can't make that journey without long rest stops that we can't afford to take. We'll need to switch mounts along the route. That's where I can help the most. I'll know what to look for in a stable and how to haggle without raising suspicions that we're easy pickings for bandits. Besides," he added with a huff, "the prince ordered me to stay by your side."

Taryn was too relieved at the idea of having a companion for his ride that he didn't try to argue the point. "We'll have to wait until nightfall." He hated losing any amount of time, but his escape had to be done under cover of darkness.

"Just as well," Nora replied. "We need to time to work out the details."

"I'll get what you'll need for traveling supplies," Deward ventured. Then he frowned. "But the guards?"

A determined look came over Nora's face. "Leave them to me."

* * * *

Taryn had spent the afternoon preparing for his journey by studying the map. He needed to be able to find Soren on his own in case something prohibited Kexen from coming along or staying with him. Now he and his groomer were finishing up their saddlebags. Some food, water and coin were all that they would be bringing. There was no point in burdening their horses with more when there would be no stopping longer than the time it took to relieve themselves, eat a quick meal or buy fresh mounts. The clothes on their backs would suffice for the entire ride. Kexen had toned down his look to a non-descript servant, and Deward had found Taryn clothes fit for a young nobleman. Gone was Taryn's unique bi-gender style, replaced with purely masculine attire that would allow him freedom of movement. Both he and Kexen wore their hair in a no-nonsense braid, and long knives hung from their belts. Taryn knew how to use one. He'd been raised as a typical Marsher boy until his father had given up hope that he would make a good soldier. Gods protect him, he didn't want to have to use it. But if that was the price of getting to Soren in time…

Taryn watched as Kexen rolled up a small flag and stuck it through the clasp of his saddlebag. "What is that?"

"The prince's standard. It will announce who we are better than any shout. We don't want to go all that way only to be cut down by his men." He gave Taryn a wry grin, although there was worry in his eyes.

Taryn put his hand on the boy's shoulder. "I couldn't do this without you. I have no words to express how I feel."

"I would find a way to go even without you, your grace. I am very fond of my cousin, Rolf. His life is on the line as well."

"Of course." So many men would die if they failed in their mission. Dozens of families would suffer the loss. It wasn't all about Soren, even though he was what mattered most to him. As the Duchess of Vostguard, Taryn had a duty to them all.

Kexen stared at their bags. "We've done what we can, and the sun is well down. Now, it's up to Princess Eleanora and Deward."

In the next instant, they heard a thud outside the door. It opened to reveal Nora and a young man dressed in a guard uniform dragging another one into the room. Nora quickly shut them in from prying eyes while her companion pulled rope from his belt and trussed up the unconscious guard. Then she whisked past them. "The other guard is being brought into your room. I'll check on how Deward and Philip are doing."

Kexen stepped forward to help. "Good evening, Lord Benja. I know you are always up for a prank, but this seems outside your usual one."

The boy grinned. "Princess Nora has promised Philip and me the first two dances of each ball. All we have to do is truss up the real guards and take their place for the night. By the time the next shift discovers us, you'll be long gone." He grinned again.

Taryn was aghast that more people had been brought into the plot. "What will be your punishment when you're discovered?"

Benja shrugged. "My father has the king's ear. He also has a sturdy belt and a strong arm with which to wield it. I expect sitting will be difficult for some time. But a dance with the princess is well worth it."

The princess reappeared. "Benja, go. Philip is already out there. I'll pick up the cups myself. Don't touch them. Some of the mead spilled down the sides when the guards collapsed. It's possible I overdid it a bit with the sleeping powder," she added with a grimace.

She turned her attention to Taryn. "You should go as well. The way is clear. Don't worry about these men. Deward and I will watch over them. All they'll have to deal with is a big headache and the shame of being stupid enough to drink what I offered them while they were on duty."

Taryn took a moment to pity the men then forgot them and their troubles. Their minor sacrifice had been critical. He hardened his resolve and drew a cloak over his shoulders. Grabbing his saddlebag, he motioned for Kexen to precede him. For once, the groomer took the lead. He still knew the palace better than Taryn did. They hurried into the hallway and over to the staircase that led down to the private courtyard. There was no one to see them as they sprinted through to a side gate and out into the area. Because there were always guards milling about, Kexen had them stick to the shadows. The way the boy darted from one dark spot to another convinced Taryn that this wasn't Kexen's first effort at stealth.

When they reached the stable, they crouched behind a thick tree to surveil who might be there. Taryn's heart sank when he saw a guard come around the other side of the barn, tucking his dick into his trousers. This was a man well-familiar to him and vise-versa. There was no way he could walk past him without being challenged.

Kexen tapped him on the shoulder and leaned over to whisper into his ear. "I'm going to distract him. When I lure him away from the door, get Wind Chaser and go out the side gate." He pointed in the direction to their left.

"Won't I be stopped?"

"The guards are to keep people out, not in. They're used to noblemen leaving for a night in the city. Keep the hood of your cloak up and they won't be able to recognize you. I'll follow as soon as I can." Kexen made a move to leave.

Taryn grabbed his arm. "Wait. How are you going to distract that guard?"

Kexen's teeth flashed in the gloom. "I only know one way to distract a man, your grace." With that, he was gone.

Taryn watched as Kexen sauntered up to the guard with his saddlebag casually slung over his shoulder. He looked as if he had all the time in the world, and while they were too far away for Taryn to hear what they were saying, Kexen coquettish body language made clear his intent. Taryn hated that the boy had to do this for him, but once again, he reminded himself of the stakes. With growing impatience, he waited until the two men disappeared around the side of the barn before racing as quietly as he could to his horse.

Wind Chaser gave him no trouble over the unexpected ride and even seemed eager for it. He tossed his head and snorted as Taryn tacked him up. With a pat on his horse's neck, Taryn flipped his hood up to hide his face as much as possible. He led his horse out of the barn and far enough away that he felt comfortable mounting him without disturbing the guard. That was assuming Kexen's 'distraction' allowed the man to hear anything at all.

Taryn's heart thumped wildly as he approached the gate at a slow trot. As Kexen had promised, however, the men stationed there gave him no scrutiny. He passed them without incident, and when he reached the cobbled road leading down into the city, kicked Wind Chaser into a faster trot. In the outskirts, he raised the pace to a canter, and whisked by the guards at another side gate out of the city. On the main roadway, he gave Wind Chaser his head and raced as fast as his horse's legs could carry him.

The sudden sense of freedom caught him by surprise. For the first time in perhaps his whole life, his destiny was in his hands and no one else's. With the coin in his saddlebag, he could afford to go anywhere and create a new life for himself. He let his imagination run wild for a few seconds before letting the fanciful idea go. His life was with Soren now, and given the choice, he wanted no other. Getting to his husband's side in time was all that mattered. He had to succeed because the thought of living without the man was intolerable.

I'm coming for you, my love.

Taryn urged Wind Chaser to go faster, slowing only as he heard galloping hooves behind him. When Kexen reached him, Taryn's heart leaped with renewed hope. Then he picked up the pace, determined that they should not fail.

* * * *

Soren drummed his fingers on his thigh as he studied the tall cliffs in the distance. "No sign of the Marshers being near, then?"

"None, your highness," Rolf confirmed. "The scouts all agree that the tracks are at least three days' old, even on the other side of the canyon. There is no trace that they stopped to make camp once they cleared their border. They'd turned tail and ran, apparently."

"Hmm, that does fit with what we know about them. Still…" Soren took a step closer as if he could somehow see anything his scouts had missed. It was ridiculous, really. He trusted their skills completely. They had the unenviable task of being the point of the army, the first to get killed if they ran into an ambush. Volunteers, every one of them, they were stealthy and clever, missing no trick. So how come the hairs on the back of his neck were standing up?

"Why here?" It didn't make any sense for the Marshers to attack from this part of the border, and that narrow canyon was the perfect place to get trapped either coming or going. He looked up. "No signs that they are on top of the cliffs?"

"None, sir. The scouts say there's nothing to indicate ladders were used on either side of the cliffs or either end of the canyon. The vegetation grows very thick all around but nothing strong enough to climb. We both know that Hogard and Hobart are dumb as rocks. Maybe we are allotting them more cunning than they deserve."

"It's certainly tempting to think that." Soren had a decision to make, and really, there was only one path forward, literally and figuratively. He couldn't afford to give the Marshers more time to mount another attack on a different part of the border. His unnamed worry had to be put aside. There was no other choice than the obvious one. "Mount up and get the men ready to march."

* * * *

Taryn nearly wept at the sight of his husband's encampment. He knew that it was a mixture of relief, exhaustion and hunger—having slept and eaten very little on his journey. The strange mount under him snorted and tested his control, as they all had done. But his mastery of horses had stood him well, and Kexen had secured strong, fast beasts at every change they made.

"We did it! We're in time." Even as he crowed the words, he could see that the army was getting ready to move. "Barely." The thought that they could have missed it by only an hour or two caused his empty stomach to cramp. He ignored it because that hadn't happened, and he only needed to find a little bit more strength, then Soren would figure out the rest.

Beside him, Kexen barked out a laugh as he unfurled the flag he'd brought. "Now all we need to do is get through the prince's men intact. Follow me, your grace." With that, the groomer put his reins between his teeth and kicked his horse into a gallop. As he headed straight for the crowd of soldiers, he stood in his stirrups and held the flag high in the air. Taryn had never seen anyone ride like that. He only spared a second to admire Kexen's skill and bravery before taking off in his wake.

* * * *

"What is that ruckus among the men?" Soren frowned as he wheeled his horse to face his soldiers.

At the same time, Rolf exclaimed, "Holy shit!" The liegeman rarely swore. Nevertheless, it was the right thing to say.

Soren stared wide-eyed as his men parted quickly to let two riders through. The first one held his banner aloft in an impressive show of horsemanship. But it was the one behind him that captured and held Soren's attention. He kicked his horse into gear with his next breath and overtook Kexen to come along side Taryn. His wife slowed his mount and they circled each other, their horses balking at the sudden movements.

It took Soren a few turns to find his voice. "Gods help me, what are you—?"

Taryn yelled over him. "It's a trap!" Then he burst into tears.

* * * *

"How long have I been asleep?"

Soren hurried to his wife's side and helped him sit up. "A few hours. Here... Have some water." He held the cup to Taryn's lips. "Kexen said you've eaten little in recent days, so Sam has left food for you when you feel up to it."

Taryn flopped back onto the pallet. "Thank you. The water is the best thing I've tasted on this journey. I'll eat soon. I need some more time to raise the energy." He looked under the light blanket and frowned. "Did Sam undress and wash me while I slept?"

Soren shook his head. "I did."

"That couldn't have been pleasant. I'd been wearing those clothes for days."

"I know. Kexen is sleeping now, but he told me all about it while he ate."

"I should have been the one to explain. I'm sorry I collapsed so completely."

Soren brushed some strands of hair away from Taryn's face. "You had good reason. To come so far so quickly was an amazing feat." And if he thought about what his bride had gone through to get to him, it would drive him mad with worry. He kept reminding himself that Taryn was here, safe with him, not lying with his throat slit by bandits on the road.

Tears rose in Taryn's eyes. "We were nearly too late."

"Hush, my love. You came in time, and I am grateful beyond words that you did. I sensed something was wrong, but we couldn't see how they might have laid a trap. Once we knew what to look for, my scouts soon found the cave openings among the vegetation. We can sneak up on them now and turn the tables, thanks to you."

"And Kexen. And Nora, Deward and those two young lords eager to dance with her at the balls. Please tell me everyone is going to be all right? The king must be furious."

"He might be if he even knows what's happened. I have a feeling that Tost will keep that information to himself. It will be seen as his failure."

"Nora told him what I knew, and he wouldn't listen."

Soren understood this already, and the only thing that tempered his fury was the sure knowledge that the minister would be living out the rest of his days in some backwater post. Soren would see to it. "Don't worry about anything, my dear. You've done what you can, and the rest is up to me."

Taryn pushed to a sitting position and reached for the tray of food. The way his loose hair framed his lovely face and how the blanket allowed some of his hips to peep out gave Soren bad ideas—ones he couldn't act on. There was a battle to be fought, and although he'd had a makeshift tent raised for Taryn's privacy, it was only four thin pieces of material and an open top. As much noise as his men were making, anything he did with his wife would still be overheard. He didn't want to embarrass Taryn now any more than he had on their original journey back to the palace. His cock would have to wait.

Taryn swallowed his mouthful of bread and cheese. "What are you going to do?"

Soren sat back on his hands. "I have the men making a show of readying once more to march, in case we are being watched from afar. If we are, they'll have seen you and Kexen riding in, but they couldn't possibly identify you, so we'll let them assume we've received some missive from my brother."

"I'm not even sure my father and brother would remember talking about this place in front of me. They mostly treated me like furniture—and unwanted at that."

Soren stayed the impulse to reach for his bride. The boy needed no distraction from his ravenous eating. "More fools they. Normally, I would hate that they treated you thusly. In this case, I can only be glad. My men would have been sitting ducks in that canyon."

Taryn nodded as he chewed. "There will be archers."

Soren was touched that his wife was still looking out for him. "I know. We have our own, and they will be backed by swords. We'll block every escape route, too. Those on the cliffs will either surrender or die. I'm sorry."

Taryn froze. "About what?"

"That I'm going to have to kill so many of your people. I'll give quarter if asked, but otherwise, there will be no mercy."

Taryn shook his head before taking a bite of an apple. "They're not my people anymore. I am a member of the royal family of Moorcondia. My loyalty is to you."

"But your heart is surely with your father's men, if not with him and your brother themselves."

Taryn looked down and said nothing for long seconds. Then he lifted his head and stared into Soren's eyes. "My heart is with you."

He saw it in his wife's eyes. Love. That was a look he was familiar with and one he hadn't expected to see directed at him again. And he could feel it rising in his own heart. Their strange marriage of convenience had turned into a love match after all. Soren smiled. "Taryn."

He didn't get a chance to say more. Rolf stuck his head in. "Your pardon, sir. We need your counsel."

"Very well, I'm coming." Soren reluctantly rose, then stole a quick kiss before moving toward the tent flap. "I am tempted to have you escorted back but you need more rest, and it will be easier to protect you here."

"I'm not afraid for myself, Soren. I only want you back hale and hearty. Will you do that for me, please?"

"I will, yes." He made it a solemn vow to himself. He would return to his bride so that they could make a happy life together. "Ah, here's Kexen."

The ever-loyal groomer came in as he lifted the flap to leave. The boy bowed. "Your highness."

Soren clapped him on his shoulder. "You are a man of great worth, Kexen of the Outer Vale. Anything you want is yours."

Kexen's gaze slid over to Taryn before he said, "The duchess is safe, and you're forewarned. I have everything I want."

"Nevertheless, we will speak of this again later." With that, Soren left the tent, determined to bring the Marshers to heel and hoping he could do so without killing Taryn's kin.

* * * *

Taryn smoothed the skirt of his simple green kirtle. "You are a clever one, Kexen, managing to secret these clothes for me in your saddle bag."

"I had a feeling they might come in handy. We can't have the Duchess of Vostguard parading about the prince's men dressed like a dirty boy after our long journey."

Taryn turned to his groomer and gave him a hug, something he'd been wanting to do since before they'd left the palace. "It's perfect, and you are priceless."

Kexen hugged him back briefly before stepping away. "Serving you is my great pleasure, your grace. And I'll be dining out on the tale of this adventure for the rest of my days," he added with a cocky grin. "Are you sure you don't want me to braid your hair?"

Taryn tossed his head. "I want it down for this."

He hesitated a second before leaving the tent. All around him, tired but cheery men milled. As they caught sight of him, they stopped their movement and their chatter. To a man, they bowed low as he passed. Taryn couldn't take the time to appreciate the show of honor and deference. He had to keep his focus on the task at hand. The battle was over, and Soren was both victorious and alive. All that remained was a decision as to what to do next. Taryn was surprised, although he shouldn't be, that his husband had asked him to join in the discussion. Soren's concern for him and his feelings was indicative of the type of man he was.

As he approached the area where the prisoners were being kept, he was surprised to see so many. Soren had kept his word, that had been a given. But he wouldn't have predicted that so many Marshers had chosen capture over death. Maybe they'd grown weary of his father's brutal and futile rule. If so, it boded well for everyone. They certainly looked downtrodden as they sat with their hands tied and their heads bowed. Much farther away from them, Soren stood with a group of his men, dirty and a bit bloody, although without obvious injury to himself. It upset Taryn to see his husband in such a condition, but he'd known he was a man to lead from the front.

Taryn's focus on Soren was derailed by the sight of his brother kneeling in the middle of the small group of Moorcondians, Sir Rolf standing behind him. Hobart's hands were bound in front of him, a courtesy to his rank. Taryn wanted to scream for Sir Rolf to watch out. His brother was a snake ready to strike. It was a good thing he'd been separated from his men. He could see the sneer on his face as he trained his gaze on Taryn's approach.

"Don't you make a pretty sight, *cunt*."

A dozen men stepped toward him with their hands on their hilts. But it was Sir Rolf who had the pleasure of responding. He slapped the back of Hobart's head. "Show our duchess respect, or we'll cut out your tongue." The usually calm man said this with such venom that Taryn believed him. So did Hobart apparently, as he fell silent and settled for showing contempt in his expression.

Ignoring him, Taryn went to Soren. "You sent for me?"

Soren's gaze was both loving and approving. It instantly calmed Taryn and gave him strength to draw on. "Yes, my dear. I seek your counsel on what to do with your brother."

Taryn didn't bother to look in Hobart's direction when the man gasped his outrage. "I am honored to give it, and it's simple." He took a deep breath and hardened his heart before he said what needed to be. "You can never trust him. No new treaty can be hacked out with him. Whatever promises he makes, he'll break them. So will my father, as long as he has Hobart by his side to do his dirty work for him. Hogard is an aging drunkard. He's cunning and duplicitous, but also inherently lazy. Without an heir, he can be managed.

"Hobart's son is only five, so no threat as of now, and he can be taught to be better than his father, I hope. Other than him, I am the only other male in the line of succession, and you know where my loyalties lie."

Soren nodded his approval. "Indeed I do. I also agree with your assessment. The question remains, what should I do with your brother?"

Taryn looked at his brother once more, saw the hatred in his eyes and was tempted to return the sentiment. He simply couldn't. "My head says to execute him here and now, a good lesson for the others and an end to the threat he poses. But my heart says to let him live and lock him in a hole somewhere for the rest of his life."

Soren didn't respond right away. Instead, he tucked some of Taryn's hair behind his ears, the touch another balm to Taryn's nerves. "If that is your wish, I am inclined to indulge you." He swung his head from side-to-side to take in the men around him before fixing on Hobart. "My wife is a compassionate person, and as he saved our lives this day, I hereby decree as Prince Soren of Moorcondia, Duke of Vostguard, that the life of Hobart of the Marshlands is spared. He will be imprisoned for the rest of his days, and may the gods grant him the wisdom to see the folly of what he wrought."

Hobart didn't appreciate the boon given. With his face bright red with his anger, he spewed his venom. "You think I care about your mercy, *brother*? It's just another sign of your weakness, not that I expect anything less from a bastard."

It took Taryn a moment to realize Hobart was speaking literally. "What is this?" In some sense, he didn't want to hear the answer, and yet he needed to.

"Our mother fucked that tinker years ago, the price for her precious fabric, no doubt. Father knew the second he laid eyes on you that you weren't his. With each passing year, that fact was more obvious. You are not a Marsher of any worth. I'm surprised father didn't kill you and her outright, but every beating he gave you both was well-deserved."

Taryn tried not to show his feelings. This knowledge wasn't a big surprise, not when he could see himself how little he resembled his kinsmen. His heart ached all over again for his mother's life and death. He was sure she'd lain with the tinker for some comfort, not simply for a scrap of silk. Hobart would never understand that this news didn't hurt Taryn. He was rather relieved to learn the truth.

"If you think this accusation changes anything, you're as stupid as I've always believed. I'm still the legal son of a chieftain. Any assertion to the contrary is nothing more than gossip." It was gratifying to see the disappointment on Hobart's face that he hadn't rattled Taryn. In the short time since they'd last seen each other, Taryn had grown strong. Hobart wouldn't have expected that, much less understood it.

Soren gave him an approving nod. "Well said, my dear. Certainly no one here would claim to have heard anything about it, in any event. The ravings of a defeated man. I promise that you won't have to listen to his ugly words ever again."

"Thank you." Taryn wanted to say more and hug his husband tightly to him. But this wasn't the time or place, and the best he could do for him was to get out of his way. "I'll wait for you in our tent." He tried to convey an invitation with his eyes alone, and from Soren's expression, he thought he'd succeeded.

Taryn turned to walk back the way he'd come, relieved that it was over for the present in any event. There was a cry of 'traitor' then a whoosh and a thud. Taryn whirled around to see Hobart's head lying severed from his body. Soren stood over him with a bloody sword in his hand. He turned his gaze toward Taryn. "He lunged for you. I couldn't take the risk."

Taryn nodded, trying not to stare at his brother's sightless eyes. "I understand." And he did, too. He still didn't manage to take another step away from the scene before the world spun and went black.

* * * *

For the second time that day, Soren sat on the ground inside their makeshift tent staring at his unconscious wife. It wasn't fair to say that Taryn slept, not when the boy had collapsed at the sight of his brother's decapitated body. *Because I swung my sword to achieve that very result.* He felt no regret over his act. Hobart had sealed his own fate when he'd tried to attack Taryn. It didn't even matter that the man could have been contained in a less lethal way. In that split second before he'd drawn his sword, all Soren could see was a future in which the Marsher man remained a threat to Soren's precious wife. The decision had been an easy one to make, except now he worried that he had forever ruined any chance of their forging a life filled with love.

Soren leaned over to brush strands of hair from Taryn's face, a habit he'd formed that he hoped never to have to break. "Will you ever forgive me for what I've done?"

"There's nothing to forgive."

Soren was momentarily taken aback, not having realized he'd asked the question out loud. He peered into his wife's now-open eyes. "How to do you feel?"

Taryn frowned. "Embarrassed."

"There is no need."

"I beg to differ. I keep fainting in front of your men."

"You've had good cause, and really, it's exhaustion from you journey here that is to blame the most. It's hard to weather a great shock when you're physically depleted."

Taryn rolled to his side to look at Soren head on. "I've seen people die before in far worse ways. And while I should feel something more this time because it was my brother" — he shrugged — "I don't. He got what he deserved, and you're safer with him gone."

Relieved that Taryn felt no animosity toward him, Soren dared to pick up his wife's hand and hold it to his chest. "You are safer, as well — and that's what counts." He paused, remembering the poison that had spewed from Hobart before his fatal mistake. "I'm sorry he was so vindictive as to throw your parentage in your face."

"I'm not." Taryn twisted his hand to lace his fingers with Soren's. "Some part of me always knew I wasn't my father's son. And I'm glad of it. Maybe that's why I could never be what he wanted. I'd like to think that my real father was Moorcondian. Do you think it's possible?"

Soren kissed the back of Taryn's hand. "I think it very likely. It explains your coloring and lack of body hair. I'm glad you want to be able to claim that parentage. I hope it makes it easier for you to settle into your new home."

"I already have. You and the girls, Kexen and everyone else who's been kind to me ensured that." He frowned and tugged his hand free. "I can tell I'm naked again. How come you aren't?"

The change in topic and the mischievous question caught Soren off guard. Then his dick hardened, and he was reaching for his belt before he realized what he was doing. "We have little privacy, my dear."

Taryn gave him smoldering look. "The sun is nearly set, and we can be very quiet. Besides, haven't you always said that the people around us like knowing we are enjoying our marriage?" Now, there was a challenge to his wife's expression.

Soren smiled slowly as he continued disrobing. "I expect I will make it very hard for you to be silent."

Taryn raised his chin. "Try me."

Soren needed no more invitation. He shucked his clothing and whipped the sheet off his bride. Taryn's cock was waiting for him, but before he could formulate a line of attack, the boy splayed his legs and lifted them. "Fuck me, Soren."

His dick nearly leaped at the idea, and it was all he could do to keep himself in check. "We have no oil."

"Use spit, like you did that time after my first ride on Wind Chaser."

He shook his head. "It's not enough. I'll hurt you as I did then and as I did our first night together."

"Now that I know how it ends with such exquisite pleasure, I don't care." Taryn's voice was fierce, and his eyes lit with passion. "I want to feel you breach me, the burn of it as your cock opens my channel to thrust as far inside as it can go. Claim me. Possess me. Remind me that I'm yours—and not because of a worthless piece of paper but because I *love* you."

Soren knew that he should say the words back to his wife. The gods knew he felt them. Yet, they stuck in his throat, constricted by a deep longing that left him incapable of speech. He could only respond in the way Taryn had pleaded for. He lay between the boy's legs and gave him what he wanted, using as much saliva as his dry mouth would allow him. The feel of Taryn's welcoming heat gripping his cock sent him over the edge after only a few thrusts. His wife came with him, bucking in his embrace and his ring squeezing Soren's shaft. He captured Taryn's mouth to catch their cries but knew they had made enough noise to announce to the world around them what they had done.

Soren didn't care. Let them listen. Let them know that Prince Soren of Moorcondia and his bride had indeed become a love match.

Epilogue

Taryn frowned at his husband through the mirror. "You've made us late."

Soren dared to laugh at him. "If I'm supposed to feel sorry for that, I can't." Putting his arms around Taryn's waist, he nuzzled his neck. "I bet I can make us even later."

Taryn slapped his hands. "Stop that!" But even as he did so, his own dick roused within his small clothes, liking the idea. And he *was* tempted. Making love to Soren was a far better way to spend the evening than at his first ball. He pressed his palm against his nervous stomach. "I can't promise I won't step on your toes tonight."

Soren backed away and turned him around so that they were face-to-face. "Given how diligent you've been in your dancing lessons, I'm not worried about that happening. Lilli says you're very good, and that's high praise indeed."

Taryn wasn't convinced. "Everyone will be watching us."

"As well they should. We are important people in this country, and you are one of the most beautiful duchesses we have. Every man will envy me, I can assure you."

"We do look particularly good this evening." They both wore dark blue velvet accented with silver piping. And this was only the first night of the ball season. There were many more, and for each one, he had an amazing ensemble, thanks to Kexen. The always-clever groomer had conspired with Deward to make sure the Duke and Duchess of Vostguard cut an elegant and coordinated appearance.

"Indeed, we do. And everyone there will wish us well. Never forget that you are a national hero."

Being uncomfortable with all the attention he'd received since returning to the palace, Taryn waved that statement away. "I am no such thing. It's enough that the war is over." As he'd predicted, without Hobart, Hogard had capitulated quickly. "That's assuming Minister Tost and my father don't start a new one between them."

Soren laughed. "I'm sure Tost is doing his best to adjust to his new position as the king's special envoy to the Marshlands. But if it does come to blows, I predict they'll kill each other with their well-matched inflated pride and stupidity."

"As long as you don't have to go sort matters out." Taryn couldn't quite shake his fear for his husband — the husband that he loved. It didn't matter if Soren hadn't said the words back to him. It was enough that the man showed his devotion every day in small ways.

"I promise you that won't happen. Now, we should go, but if we're very clever, we might be able to sneak out early. Come, my dear," he added reaching for him.

"I am reassured on both counts, then." He started to take Soren's proffered hand then stopped. "Wait. I have something for you."

He'd intended many times since returning to give Soren his wedding ring. Somehow the time had never felt right. This night, however, was the perfect occasion. He wanted everyone to see how good his marriage had become. Crossing to his nightstand, he pulled open the drawer where he'd moved it to keep it close. He took the box out and brought it back to an openly curious Soren.

Suddenly shy, Taryn hesitated before opening the box and holding it out for his husband to see. "I would be honored if you would wear this."

Soren stared at him for agonizingly long seconds, saying nothing, and not reaching for the ring. Just as Taryn feared he'd made a mistake, his husband pulled him in for a crushing kiss that left Taryn reeling. He was still trying to gather his scattered thoughts again when Soren released his lips.

Soren plucked the box from Taryn's nerveless fingers, took out the ring and tossed the box aside. "It's priceless."

Taryn blinked to clear his vision. "Well, it was rather expensive, but it's only platinum and onyx."

"Those are things, Taryn. It's the sentiment behind your giving this to me that is beyond measure. I can't tell you how touched I am. Will you please put it on me?"

Relieved and excited in equal measure, Taryn did as he'd been asked. When he slipped the ring onto his husband's finger, he felt their bond stronger than at any time during sex. This band of metal was a symbol of their union that would remain, even if age ever robbed them of their passion.

"I love you, Soren," he said simply, staring into his eyes. "I want everyone to know that."

His husband cupped his chin and kissed him as gently as he'd ever done. "I love you, as well, my sweet bride. I should have told you a long time ago."

The way Taryn felt, as if his feet floated off the floor, he was sure he would have no trouble dancing now. "Oh, Soren, you've told me when I needed to hear it the most. Let's go show the court how good a marriage a Moorcondian prince and a Marsher boy can make."

Soren took his hand. "Indeed, we will."

Later, as his husband took him in his arms to dance for the first time in front of the entire court, Taryn finally gave in to his happiness, sure that it would never leave him — not when Soren was there to remind him that he was loved.

Want to see more from this author?
Here's a taster for you to enjoy!

Treaty Brides:
The Diplomat's Bride
Samantha Cayto

Coming June 2022

Excerpt

Benedict, Lord Tentrees of Northcliff, stood at the balcony's rail and peered down at the colorful spectacle of the servants' ball. Technically, he had no business being there. The ball season for the nobility had already ended earlier in the evening. These final hours were intended to benefit those who served the palace denizens so faithfully throughout the year. This was a grand gesture of thanks for their hard work and loyalty. Woe be it to anyone who didn't give a servant these few hours to enjoy themselves with food, drink and merriment. The royal family had long made it clear that this was by decree. There would be some aching heads and sleepy eyes come the harsh light of the morning, but for now, the people twirling around the dance floor and taking liberties with each other in corners had no care in the world—or so it seemed to him. Not that his gaze landed on anyone for long, because he was there to find one person in particular.

It wasn't difficult for him to spot his quarry. Even among the bright garments of the attendants, Kexen of the Outer Vale stood out. He was clothed in the colors of fall—deep red, bright orange and sparkling yellow. His daringly short doublet sported gathered sleeves that cascaded in folds down his slender arms while provocatively highlighting what lay behind the crotch of his almost obscenely snug trousers. His knee-high brown leather boots gave his legs an even longer look, while his elaborately braided hair swung with his every graceful turn. Kexen was not a tall man, but that was all to the good. The boy would fit perfectly with Ben's own height. The vision of gathering him in his arms was captivating. His cock hardened at the thought of it, enjoying the spark of pleasure. With his demanding profession, there wasn't much opportunity to slake his needs. Hopefully, that situation was about to change.

There was no reason to tarry any longer, so, stepping away from his vantage point, he headed toward the staircase that would send him into the midst of the revelers. He had intended to be as inconspicuous as possible, understanding that this was not his domain, that he was an interloper who might cause some alarm among the servants. His good intentions notwithstanding, the severity of his all-black clothing served to make him stand out among the festive outfits of those around him. There was a certain amount of startlement by those who saw and recognized his station, if not his identity, leading to smiles morphing into more respectful expressions. Some nodding of heads occurred, as well, in deference to his rank. Ben tried to convey that he was no threat to them, that he had no demands, not even any expectations—not from these people, in any event. Kexen was a different story altogether. If all went to plan, Ben would seduce the boy while judging up close whether they would make a good match.

Ben caught sight of Kexen on the dance floor again. He was being whirled around in the beefy arms of a footman. Ben settled against the wall to stay unobtrusive as he waited with less patience than he would have expected from himself for the musicians to end their song. The moment the last of the notes were played, he launched into the crowd. Now he appreciated being shown respect as the partying servants cleared a way for him, making his journey that much quicker. He caught up with Kexen and his partner just as they were stepping out onto one of the balconies. The night was brisk but, in contrast to the heat of the ballroom, very refreshing — not that the cold air served to dampen his ardor. Seeing Kexen up close only increased his desire for the boy.

Exquisite.

Kexen's face was lit with joviality as he gazed up at the footman, laughing at something the man had said. There was a coy look to the boy's expression, as well. Ben was surprised at the spurt of jealousy he felt at the sight. He reminded himself that Kexen was not his and might never be so unless he proved to be worthy. Charging forth as if he were an enraged lover was hardly going to serve that purpose. Being a diplomat, he knew how to bank his emotions and measure his words and actions. By the time he reached the couple, he hoped he appeared friendly and casual.

Kexen was the first to spot him. His jubilance dimmed somewhat, although he looked more curious than apprehensive. He nodded his head. "My lord, is there something you wish?"

You. In my bed. Ben didn't voice this desire out loud, of course. Instead, he said, "I would love a dance, if you would honor me." Ben had the pleasure of seeing surprise flash across the boy's face. He was delighted that the obviously confident young man could still be caught off guard.

Kexen reached to twist one finger around the chain of a small ruby pendant and dropped his gaze. "I am honored, my lord. But your pardon, this is the servants' ball. It is not fit for a nobleman." Just as Ben was appreciating the subtlety of the rebuke, Kexen looked up at him from under his lashes.

Cheeky boy, you're interested. Ben stepped closer. "And a fine event it is. Please forgive the intrusion, but I have been anticipating the opportunity to meet you, Kexen of the Outer Vale. This seemed the best occasion to do so."

Now Kexen showed open welcome, his lips curling in a beckoning smile. "Oh. You flatter me, my lord."

The footman proved that his brains weren't as big as his muscles. When the man opened his mouth as if to object, Ben stepped deftly between him and Kexen and stared the footman down. "If you don't mind?"

They were matched in height, and while Ben wasn't quite as broad, he could hold his own in a brawl as well as at the negotiation table — not that either skill was required in this event. He didn't hesitate to convey his social position in his gaze to encourage the footman to find someone else to dally with. The man was confident but not entirely stupid, apparently. With a curt nod, he strode away.

Pleased with the outcome, Ben turned to Kexen and held out his hand. "They are playing a waltz...my favorite."

Kexen managed to convey shyness, something his reputation belied. Ben didn't mind the pretext. The boy's ability to navigate the complex waters of a court was one of the things that Ben coveted him for. He hadn't been worried about a refusal, but when Kexen put his hand in his own, the jolt of excitement Ben felt was a surprise. He prided himself on being cool and measured in his actions. Something about the feel of this boy, however, made him want to drag him off into a corner and do a different kind of dance—one that involved his cock sliding past those slightly tinted and lovely lips. The way Kexen closed the distance between them, wrapping his arm around Ben's neck, told him that the boy had similar ideas. Such a temptation, but Ben schooled himself to be patient, because this night was not a one-time seduction. It was hopefully the beginning of a short courtship.

Ben took his dance partner by the waist and pulled him in close, letting Kexen feel the measure of his arousal. "Let us stay out here. I wouldn't want my presence to impede the others' enjoyment. I will endeavor to keep you warm." So saying, he began to slowly lead the boy in circles.

Kexen tilted his head to look him in the eye. "You are succeeding admirably, my lord."

"I'm gratified to hear it. I'm Benedict, by the way."

"I know who you are, Lord Tentrees. I must confess to being surprised that you know who I am."

Ben whirled them into the far recesses of the balcony, taking them away from everyone else. "You shouldn't be. Who at the palace hasn't heard of the valiant groomer of the Duchess of Vostguard? You helped to save Prince Soren from an ambush at grave risk to your own safety."

Kexen dropped his gaze and shrugged. "Oh, that. It was all the Duchess' doing. I merely went along to serve him, as is my duty."

Ben knew false modesty when he heard it, and this was decidedly *not* that. Kexen truly believed his actions weren't worthy of special mention. Ben's estimation of him increased. There was more to this boy than beauty and even bravery. Most people in his position would brag to anyone and everyone about such exploits, not caring if their words betrayed the secrets of those whom they served. Kexen's humbleness and discretion were excellent traits in diplomatic circles. There was no doubt in Ben's mind that he had made the right choice, even if it were really the only one afforded him.

"You don't do yourself justice. I've attended a few meetings in the presence of the king. I assure you he feels quite differently."

Kexen blushed despite the cold air swirling around them. "The royal family is very kind, my lord."

"My friends call me Ben."

"I am surely not that upon such a short acquaintance."

"I should like you to be." He let his passion show in his eyes. "Should we continue our dance somewhere more private inside?" He actually held his breath waiting for the reply. In theory, he could have his way whether Kexen wanted him or not. King Auden didn't tolerate the abuse of servants, but pressure could be brought to bear quietly against even the most secure servants with little retribution, if one was careful about it. But that wasn't how he intended this venture to go. An eager Kexen would be a far better prize than a reluctant and begrudging one.

Kexen rested his cheek on Ben's shoulder. "I would like that very much."

Ben wasted no time, ending their dance before tugging Kexen by the hand back into the ballroom. He skirted the crowd to leave through the nearest exit and led the boy to the first quiet alcove he could find. The palace had so many discreet places for assignations that he was inclined to believe it was by deliberate design. Part of him disliked being so public. He would have preferred to take Kexen back to his own apartment, but, despite his recent promotion in the diplomatic corps, he still didn't have a room in the palace. Taking the time to dress for outside and head to his place in the city didn't appeal to him. Plus, he didn't want to burden Kexen with two trips — there and back — on such a cold and late night.

The moment they were out of the sight of prying eyes, he pulled the boy into a kiss. He'd intended to take it slowly, to do nothing that might alarm even an experienced person such as Kexen. One touch of their lips, however, had him devouring the boy's mouth instead. His much-valued control snapped with a speed that alarmed him. Or, rather, it would have, if feasting on Kexen were not as delectable as it was. Within seconds, he was sitting on a tufted settee with Kexen straddling his lap. Their respective erections mashed against each other as much as their clothing allowed. Ben wanted nothing more than to strip those barriers away. He had to wrestle with himself to gain control over his passion.

Breaking the kiss, he peppered Kexen's jaw with quick pecks. "We must slow down, my dear, or I won't last much longer."

Kexen giggled in a sweet voice. "Who says I want you to...*Ben*?"

Hearing his name spoken in a voice thick with need nearly sent him over the edge. He closed his eyes and nuzzled the side of the boy's neck, breathing in the sharp scent of bergamot mixed with the more musky smell of his arousal. As Ben worried that his mind was becoming cloudy, Kexen slipped from his grasp and was kneeling between his legs before Ben knew what was happening.

"Let me make you happy." That was all the boy said before undoing the laces of Ben's trousers, freeing his cock.

What rational thought that was left in his mind fled in the next instance when Kexen swallowed him whole right down nearly to the root. It was an impressive feat based on his prior experience. No one had ever taken the entirety of his rather large dick, and few had been able to manage as much as Kexen was now. The intensity of being mostly encased in such tight, wet heat nearly undid him. Then Kexen worked his throat muscles to massage the top half of Ben's shaft. That was all it took for him to double over from his orgasm, pressing his lips tight to keep from shouting his pleasure.

Kexen kept lavishing attention on Ben's dick until it popped out of his mouth. The boy beamed up at him as Ben caught his breath. "Do you feel better now, my lord?"

By way of an answer, Ben hauled him back up to his lap with a swiftness that made Kexen gasp. "Not nearly enough. I want more." He kissed the boy again, tasting his own bitterness. Far from being disgusted, he loved it, because it was a mingling of them both. He wanted to reciprocate the giving of such pleasure. But when he reached between them to cup Kexen's erection, he found that the boy had already come from the cocksucking alone. Knowing that he'd had such a potent effect on him puffed up his chest. He wondered if he could do it again and found himself eager to try. There was plenty of time left in the night, and based on the way Kexen melted into his arms, he seemed just as eager for more.

This was proof that he'd been right all along. Kexen of the Outer Vale was the perfect bride for him.

* * * *

"Ow!" The Duchess of Vostguard put his hand to his head as he frowned at Kexen through his reflection in the mirror. "What has my hair done to offend you this morning?"

Mortified, Kexen hurried to make amends. "I beg your pardon, Your Grace. I'm all sixes and sevens today."

"So I have observed." The duchess grinned. "I suppose the servants' ball went to the wee hours. I'm not surprised you're tired. Thank the gods the season is over. I don't think I could stand another night of feasting and dancing. Such a waste," he added with a shake of his head. Being a Marsher by birth, the man was still not used to the excesses of the Moorcondian palace.

Kexen resumed brushing his head, more careful in dealing with the snarls. He'd been woolgathering, reliving the exquisite and all-too-short time he'd shared with Lord Tentrees and hoping it hadn't been a gentle form of dismissal when the man had sent him off to bed with promises of them seeing each other again. The mere thought of kissing the nobleman and more sent Kexen's body into a state of painful arousal. He'd been careful to wear loose trousers and a long tunic, both to ease his aching cock and to hide his undiminished happiness. The duchess didn't need a hard shaft poking the back of his head.

Kexen made idle chit-chat to take his mind off the previous night's pleasures. "All will be relatively quiet for a while now until the snow comes. Then it will be time for the winter festival. It goes on in various ways until spring. There's so much fun to be had." Satisfied with the silky fall of his duchess's hair, he began to plait it in the simple style his master preferred.

The duchess grinned. "I am looking forward to that, actually. Occasionally we get a light frost in the Marshlands, but I've never truly experienced snow."

Kexen smiled at the man's reflection. "I think you will love the sporting events, and there are sleigh rides and ice skating, hot chocolate by the barrelful and flavored treats made out of shaved ice. I'm sure the prince is looking forward to introducing you to all of it."

"I expect you're right. Soren says he loves experiencing everything through my eyes. It makes it fresh for him."

Kexen scrutinized his work and, satisfied, stood back to let the duchess rise to be dressed. "You and the prince can still ride, too. Moorcondian steeds are used to prancing through the snow."

"So I've heard. It's sounds very exciting." The duchess stood still as Kexen removed his robe and began to dress him for the day. While it was obvious to him that the duchess was still not comfortable with being pampered in such a way, they'd developed a good rhythm in handling it. "That reminds me, Kexen. The prince has had a delivery of horses for you to choose from."

This news was not unexpected, and while he was excited at the prospect of gaining a new mount, he was also becoming embarrassed at the gifts being showered on him by the royal couple. "Oh, Your Grace, you'll spoil me. It's truly not necessary." Kexen turned the man so that he could see his reflection in the long mirror. The duchess's mode of dress was quite simple, being a long kirtle with matching trousers. There would be less fun to be had in choosing his outfits now that the ball season was over, although they'd barely started planning out the winter wardrobe. That was something exciting to look forward to.

The duchess turned this way and that before saying, "We're going to have to disagree on that point, Kexen. There aren't enough gifts in the world for me to show how much I value what you've done for me and my husband. Soren feels the same way." He turned to grin at him directly. "You're just going to have to get used to being spoiled."

Kexen returned the look and sighed dramatically. "I suppose I'll manage." When the duchess stood scrutinizing him, he asked, "What is it, Your Grace?"

"I don't know exactly. You seem particularly...*satisfied* this morning. And your mind has been elsewhere. I suppose you dallied with an especially appealing man at the ball?"

Kexen's cheeks heated with embarrassment. It wasn't like him to be so when the issue of men arose. And because he'd developed something of a friendship with the duchess and trusted him entirely, he readily confessed that it was true. "I did, as it happens. A nobleman," he added in a low voice as if it were a great secret.

The duchess raised his eyebrows. "What was a nobleman doing at the servants' ball?"

"Looking for me, or so he said." The fact that such a dashing man as Benedict had sought him out especially was astounding to him and made him want to preen with pride.

"Who was it?"

"Lord Tentrees…the diplomat," he added.

The duchess pursed his lips. "I know of him. We've been introduced, at least, and I believe I've heard that he's doing quite well in service to the king. He's very handsome, too, is he not?"

Kexen grinned broadly. "Yes, he is. And he's not some soft nobleman. I could feel the strength of his muscles as I held on to him." He didn't add that the man had been blessed with a long, thick cock. The duchess wasn't comfortable with such frank talk.

"Hmm-m. I suppose there's no harm in it, so long as you had a good time. Be careful, though. I don't like the idea of these noblemen taking advantage of you, Kexen."

"Be at ease about that, Your Grace. Lord Tentrees was every bit a gentleman, and I probably won't even see him again." That last thought made him sad. Funny, that. He wasn't one to pine after any one man. There was something different about Benedict, however. *Ben.* He had said they were friends. Kexen could only hope that would prove to be true.

About the Author

Samantha Cayto is a Boston-area native who practices as a business lawyer by day while writing erotic romance at night—the steamier the better. She likes to push the envelope when it comes to writing about passion and is delighted other women agree that guy-on-guy sex is the hottest ever.

She lives a typical suburban life with her husband, three kids and four dogs. Her children don't understand why they can't read what she writes, but her husband is always willing to lend her a hand—and anything else—when she needs to choreograph a scene.

Samantha loves to hear from readers. You can find her contact information, website details and author profile page at https://www.pride-publishing.com

PUBLISHING

Sign up for our newsletter and find out about all our romance book releases, eBook sales and promotions, sneak peeks and FREE romance books!